Pansy
and the
Promise

STANLEY ROSS RULE

Illustrated by Rebecca D. Miller

WESTBOW®
PRESS
A DIVISION OF THOMAS NELSON
& ZONDERVAN

The italicized words in the story are further defined in the glossary.

Scripture taken from the King James Version of the Bible.

Scripture quotations are from The Holy Bible, English Standard Version® (ESV®), copyright © 2001 by Crossway, a publishing ministry of Good News Publishers. Used by permission. All rights reserved.

WestBow Press books may be ordered through booksellers or by contacting:

WestBow Press
A Division of Thomas Nelson & Zondervan
1663 Liberty Drive
Bloomington, IN 47403
www.westbowpress.com
1 (866) 928-1240

ISBN: 978-1-4908-5634-6 (sc)
ISBN: 978-1-4908-5635-3 (hc)
ISBN: 978-1-4908-5633-9 (e)

Library of Congress Control Number: 2014918624

Printed in the United States of America.

WestBow Press rev. date: 10/29/2014

Dedicated to my Grandchildren

Annie

Rosalan

Mark

Alissa

Emily

Hailey

Madison

Bethany

Hadley

Jackson

and all that will follow.

Lulu
Always remember to
Trust the Lord

"... For He has said, 'I will never leave you, nor forsake you.'"

Hebrews 13:5 English Standard Version

Acknowledgements

I would like to thank the love of my life, my wife and best friend, Judy, for her many contributions to this work. Her expertise as an elementary teacher for thirty years aided in keeping my writing aimed and at the appropriate age level. Her support as a wife kept me focused and encouraged. Her love and understanding for Grandmother Pansy helped me remember that my desire to pass the message of her life on to our Grandchildren was a worthy task deserving of the efforts required.

****

I would like to thank Elisabeth "Betty" Scribner, better known as my sister, for hundreds of hours of editing, analysis, re-editing, reading, and re-reading to help buff up my efforts and make them readable and acceptable. Betty brings her many years of writing for the government to this more joyful and meaningful task of telling the story of our family and Grandmother Pansy's colorful and powerful life. Beyond these skills, Betty has always been the manager of this project. Her help weaving through the many issues involved in publishing and promoting the story of "Pansy" is deeply appreciated.

****

I would like to thank Ruth Rule Smith, also known as my sister, for the endless research she contributed to the development of these stories. The bulk of that research can be found in a book she published in 1986 documenting the history of the Rule/Hunt family called "The Golden Rule." Her research helped to establish credibility for the truths declared in these pages.

****

I would like to thank Artist and Illustrator, Rebecca D. Miller, who brought to life these stories in pictures. When I first approached Becky about this project, I asked if she could give this book an old-fashioned feel, as I remember in so many children's books when growing up. Her expertise with pencil and chalk goes far beyond my original vision. Becky took on this project as more than a job but, also, as a ministry. I believe her passion for the story is seen in every picture. Other books Becky has illustrated and some of her fine work in sculpture can be seen at www.boosart.com.

****

A sincere appreciation to Marian Wilbur, who so kindly volunteered to read and edit this book. Marian was an educator for 28 years, both at West Junior High School and Bishop Seabury Academy in Lawrence, Kansas. She also is an active volunteer in the Lawrence Friends of the Library. Marian and my sister, Betty, were neighbors for more than forty years in Lawrence, Kansas.

****

Thank you to Rod Hitchcock, artist of the Log Cabin Ranch House shown in Chapter 20, for an accurate portrayal of "the old home place." Mr. Hitchcock is a great-great grandson of George A. Hunt, Pansy's father.

Contents

Introduction

I set about to write this book for only one reason. I wanted my grandchildren to know the events of my Grandmother Rule's life. These stories were told to me, on the occasion of many visits to her home, as I grew up. Grandmother Rule was a master storyteller. This is a talent for which I am very grateful to have experienced personally, sitting at her feet, but one of which I am not blessed. I wish I could have passed on these narratives, as she did, to eager eyes awaiting the next tale of bygone days. Having attempted that a time or two, I thought better of it and chose to allow pen and paper to communicate, in some measure, what my grandmother's voice so adequately accomplished.

These are stories of my grandmother's life with her family, whose log cabin home still stands in the valley north of Lincoln, New Mexico, after more than one hundred years. I have been privileged to stand in that home due to the gracious kindness of its present occupants and gaze at the vast plain pouring out from the Capitan peaks behind the house. Neither my pen nor my imagination could expect to portray the experience of hearing these stories told by the one who lived them. However, my hope is to capture the essence of her message. For me, there was always a single significance behind each and every story I was told. The central point was and always will be the same. It was the promise of God, which states " . . . I will never leave you nor forsake you," (Heb. 13:5 ESV). Countless times, I have stood on Grandmother Rule's front porch after a visit to her home and, without fail, in each and every case, from the time I was a child to the last time I stood there in my late teens, she would hug me and look in my eyes, while quoting that scripture. She would then tell me, "Remember, Stanley, God promised He will never leave you nor forsake you." It was predictable as the fresh smell of flowers in her living room and the great smell of dinner in her kitchen. It was the theme of her life and the message of this narrative.

Also, I have taken certain liberties in the telling of this story, especially with regard to my grandmother's early life. I have chosen to relay the stories as my childish mind perceived them. As I have grown older, I learned that a few minor issues were a little different than I was able to understand at the time. Other family members, who were privileged to hear these tales, may remember them in a different way. Their recall may well be superior to mine, and, therefore, more accurate. My hope in the telling of these stories is not so much to recreate in exact detail the facts and events, but to communicate, in precise measure, the message grandmother was teaching.

Finally, I wish to explain the two major characters of this story. By name, they are Pansy, a nine-year-old girl, who lives on the prairie in a log house in New Mexico, and Virginia, Pansy's great aunt whom she has never met. These two characters are, in real life, one and the same –– my grandmother was Pansy Virginia Hunt Rule. The stories, which are told to Pansy as a child by her parents, are actually the true stories of what would become her later life after she moved from New Mexico with her husband, William Hiram Rule, and they started their life together in Missouri and Kansas. This specific way of telling the story of her life allows me to offer a child's perspective in the hearing of these stories much as I heard them. The one exception to this is the story of Pansy's Great-Great Grandmother Nancy Ross. I offer these memories in the hope that they will impact your faith in God and build your trust in His eternal love for you.

Chapter 1

The Visitor in the Night

Far up in the mountains of New Mexico, nestled near the area where the flat range rises to the high *Capitan* peaks, there was a log ranch house where a little girl by the name of *Pansy* lived with her mother and father.

This was prairie country, where the land stretched farther than the eye could see, and the nearest neighbor was miles down the road. This was more than one hundred years ago. It was long before such things as airplanes or cell phones or television had been invented. Cars were new and only a few rich people owned them.

Pansy loved living on the prairie in the shadow of the tall Capitan Mountains. For fun, she enjoyed playing with rag dolls Mama had made of old cloth and rag scraps or taking long walks away from the house in the prairie cactus. She loved the sweet smell of cactus blooms in the spring and the beautiful sight of the sunsets over the mountains. It was a wonderful place to live with her family.

However, it could also be a treacherous place to live. It was near the mountain forest, which meant wild animals such as bears, coyotes, and wolves were nearby and everyone had to be on guard for them. A wild animal might attack a lamb or even a young colt.

This was why Pansy's papa, as the family called him, brought a puppy to the house one day. "He will be a good watchdog," Papa said. "He is an *American bulldog*. They are ferocious fighters and, also, he will bark if anyone or anything comes close to the house." Pansy loved the puppy. She named him Star because he was black as night with just one spot of white on his forehead that looked like a shining star.

Star would sleep every night on a woven Indian rug that lay in front of the kitchen sink. During the day this was his lookout post, though most of the time he just took naps there. Star grew up quickly and looked a little scary with his wrinkled face and mighty teeth, but to Pansy, Star would always be her puppy and her friend. Any time a visitor or wild animal came near the cabin, Star would stand up quickly and begin to bark in a low, rusty voice. This would make any intruder think twice before coming closer to the house. Pansy felt safe when Star was on watch all night long.

From time to time, Pansy's papa would go to *Silver City* on business. Silver City was a two-day ride by horseback. He would saddle up his horse and take along some lunch in the saddlebag. Pansy always wanted to go along, but Papa usually told her to stay at the log cabin and help Mama with the chores. She knew he would be back in a few days.

Now, it was always a little scary, when Papa left for town, because Mama and Pansy were alone in the house all night long. One of those nights, as Pansy lay in bed, her mind began to imagine all sorts of wild animals like bears and lions coming down out of the mountains. She thought she heard the rustling of bushes outside the window and the clomp-clomp-clomp of footsteps near the house. Pansy pulled the blanket up over her head as if to hide herself from whatever she thought she heard. Clomp-clomp-clomp, she still imagined. Maybe it was only a prairie rabbit passing by . . . but what if it were a bear sneaking up on the back of the cabin or a mountain lion creeping through the woods toward the sheep!

Then Pansy remembered that Star was in the kitchen lying on the rug. She knew his keen sense of hearing would alert him to the slightest intruder outside the cabin and he would begin to bark. She listened again and could not hear the clomp-clomp-clomp. She only heard the gentle night wind over the prairie and the sound of Star sleeping on the Indian rug in the kitchen. Pansy took a deep breath, removed the blanket from over her head, and then drifted off to sleep.

Hours passed when, suddenly, the quiet of the night was shattered with the sound of BARK! BARK! Star sounded like a shot from a rifle. BARK! BARK! He woke up Mama and Pansy with a start. By the time Pansy got out of bed and put on her housecoat and slippers, Mama was already standing near the front door with a shotgun by her side. BARK! BARK! GRRRROWL! Star pointed toward the front door.

"What is it?" Pansy asked Mama.

Mama answered, "I don't know, but something has Star worried."

Mama peeked out the front window. When Papa built the log cabin, he made it with windows only in the front. Right now, Mama was wishing he had put a window in the back so she could see if something or someone was out there. It was a bright moonlit night. As Mama looked out the front window, she could see the prairie brush and the cactus, but she could not see anything or anyone moving around.

BARK!! BARK!!! Star's alarm was sounding more intense and concerned for whatever was going on outside. That's when Mama made a decision.

"I'll let Star out of the front door to chase whatever is out there," Mama said to Pansy.

"But, Mama!" Pansy protested, "What if something out there hurts Star?"

3

Mama, Pansy, and Star

"Star is a smart dog and he can take care of himself," Mama said and, with that, she lifted the large board that held the door shut. She opened the porch door, just a crack to peek out, but saw nothing. So, she opened the door a little wider, just enough for Star's powerful body to slip through. Before she could say, "Go!" Star took off like a bullet chasing out into the dark.

BARK!!! BARK!!! BARK!!! He sounded his alarm as he ran from the cabin toward a small hill just a little way from the road. He ran up over the hill. Bark!! Bark!! Bark!! Mama and Pansy could still hear Star, but the sound was fainter and farther away. "What is he doing?" they wondered.

Pansy was worried that something dreadful might happen to Star and she stood closely beside Mama as they both waited and listened. Bark, bark, bark! They could hear the faintest sound of Star still out there. Then silence. Not even the night prairie wind could be heard. It was as if everything had come to a stop. Pansy could feel her heart beating fast in her chest and Mama's grip on the old shotgun became a little tighter.

They waited by the front door for what seemed like a long, long time when, all at once, they could hear the pounding of rapidly running feet swiftly coming toward the cabin. In the moonlight, they could see the shadowy figure of a dog dashing back toward the house. It was Star returning as fast as he had left. When he came through the door, it was with so much force that it knocked Mama back on her heels, and the shotgun almost came out of her hand.

Quickly, Mama shut and barred the door. Pansy threw her arms around Star's neck. "What was it, boy?" she asked, as though the dog was going to sit back and explain what was out there in the night. Whatever happened, it was clear to both Mama and Pansy that the danger was over. Then, Star sipped some water from his bowl and curled up on the Indian rug in front of the kitchen sink, and quickly fell asleep.

The next morning, bright and early, Pansy awoke again to Star's yelp. This time, though, it was not the warning bark they had heard in the night, but the sound Star made to announce a neighbor was coming up the road toward the cabin.

Pansy scrambled from her bed just in time to hear Mama greeting the neighbor, *Mr. McCue,* from down the road. He was riding up the trail that led to the house from the main road. It was a hot, dusty day, and Pansy could see the dust puffing up from the hooves of Mr. McCue's horse.

"Hello, neighbor!" Mama greeted Mr. McCue.

"Have a little trouble here last night?" asked Mr. McCue as he tipped his hat in polite greeting.

"Why do you ask?" answered Mama.

"They shot a mountain lion down the road late last night coming from your direction, so I decided to come up this morning to the corral and check that new colt *Mr. Hunt* had tied up there. I knew he had gone to Silver City on business."

"That's mighty kind of you!" said Mama, as Pansy peeked out from behind her skirt.

Mr. McCue went on to say that he had found teeth marks on the colt's neck where some animal, probably the mountain lion, had attacked him. He said the colt was okay but something must have scared that lion away or the colt would have been killed.

Pansy spoke up, "It was Star!" She looked up at Mama for an approving glance.

"Probably so," said Mama, and she told Mr. McCue the whole story of their terrifying visitor in the night.

"That's some mighty fine dog you've got there, Pansy," said Mr. McCue. "He must have fought off that mountain lion and scared him away from the colt in the corral."

Pansy knelt beside Star and put her arms around his neck. "I think he's a hero," said Pansy. "We should do something special for him, don't you think, Mama?"

Mama smiled and said, "The best reward for Star would be a long nap, curled up on the Indian rug, in front of the sink." So that's just what he did.

Star, the Hero!

Chapter 2

Papa's Surprise

Pansy awoke when the first rays of sunlight slid through the little opening in her bedroom curtains. Every morning started early on the ranch, but today was special since Papa would be returning from Silver City. When Papa went away to the city, his return was always a special time. Mama would greet him with a warm hug and, of course, there would be a welcome home dinner with all the extras.

What Pansy looked forward to most was that time after dinner when the dishes were washed, dried, and placed back on the shelf. Then, the whole family would gather around the fireplace or sometimes out on the front porch, which overlooked the vast prairie stretched out like a carpet from the base of the mountains. Papa would tell about his trip to Silver City. He and Mama would discuss business for a while, and then they would settle back in their rocking chairs for the rest of the evening.

As the sun would settle down over the mountains to the west, Papa would tell stories about the old days with Indians and cowboys and pioneers coming to settle the land. Papa was a wonderful storyteller. This night, however, would be even more special than the rest. Papa was coming home with a big surprise for the whole family.

To Pansy, the day seemed to go on forever as she waited and watched for Papa's return. From the front of the house, she could see the pathway that stretched out for a mile down to the main road. Every now and then Pansy would look up from doing her chores, searching far down the pathway to see if she could spot Papa riding up the road on Thunder, his favorite horse. Pansy busied herself with daily duties like feeding their little flock of chickens and watering the horses penned up in the corral.

Water was an important thing at the ranch house. On the prairie, water was hard to find. Papa had built the log ranch house right next to the coldest stream rushing down out of the mountains. That was long ago before people had running water in their houses. Most people had to fetch water in a bucket and carry it to the house for washing and cleaning. Papa was very clever. He had designed a metal pipe that carried the water from the stream right into the house so they always had cold, running water when it was needed. Pansy was thankful that she did not have to carry heavy water buckets to the house like most of her school friends.

The afternoon sun was beginning to fade just a little and Pansy was cleaning out the last stall for the ponies. She was so busy, she had almost forgotten about Papa's return. Then Star, who was always nearby, stood up and barked as if to say, "Look, Pansy, someone's coming up the road!" Suddenly, she heard the familiar sound of a horse. She knew the sound of Thunder's whinny. She looked up from the pony stall and there was Papa! He was already half way up the trail leading to the ranch house from the main road.

Quickly, she shut the gate and rushed down the trail to greet Papa. "Papa!" she cried out.

"Pansy!" Papa's voice returned. As Pansy came close, Papa reached down with his big hand and scooped her up and onto the saddle. Pansy had ridden on Thunder many times with Papa. She always loved to hold the reigns and guide the horse's massive body. As they came close to the ranch house, Mama appeared on the front porch, beaming, thankful to have Papa back home.

In a moment, Papa, Mama, and Pansy were hugging and laughing on the front porch. Pansy impatiently began telling about their scary night and the mountain lion. She was talking so fast Mama had to slow her down.

"Pansy!" Mama complained, "Let your father come in and rest! There will be time for that later." They stepped into the ranch house where the warm smell of fresh baked bread and delicious food, cooking on the stove, filled the house.

Dinnertime around the ranch house table was filled with family conversation. Most of the talk was about their long night and the mountain lion that came to visit. Papa was proud of the way Mama and Pansy handled things and, especially, pleased with the way Star carried out his duties to warn and protect the family while he was gone. Star looked up from his familiar spot on the Indian rug in front of the kitchen sink when Papa said his name.

"Good boy, Star!" Papa said. Star would have come over to Papa at the table, but he was enjoying his nap too much to leave. He just opened one eye and wagged his stubby tail.

Papa suggested they all move out to the front porch after dinner. It was a beautiful night with a light breeze blowing through the prairie. He told Mama and Pansy he had a surprise for them. They were busy finishing the dishes. Around the ranch house, Papa and Mama had a strict rule. They always finished the chores, first, before relaxing or playing. Pansy knew the dishes would have to be washed, dried, and set back on the shelves before the surprise could be revealed. Somehow, she suspected that she was the only one who didn't already know what the surprise might be. Perhaps Papa had purchased something special when he was in Silver City.

When every dish was washed and put neatly away on the shelves, Mama put on her sweater and they both headed out to the front porch where Papa had just sat down in one of the rocking chairs. Pansy was all keyed up with excitement to hear the news from Papa, but he just sat there rocking and looking out over the prairie.

It was almost dark now. The only light was the flickering of an old oil lantern that gave just enough glow to dimly reveal everyone's faces. Pansy could see Papa's slight smile as he complimented Mama on a fine dinner and talked to her about the weather. Pansy was old enough to understand he was putting off telling of his big surprise just to tease her. She thought to herself, "Why do grownups think it is so much fun to keep a kid waiting for a surprise, when they can see how much the kid wants to know about the surprise?"

Finally, Papa said to everyone, "I have a surprise for you! I'm planning to take a long trip and I'm going to take both of you with me." Pansy's mind raced. A long trip for her was a buggy ride into Silver City. That would take most of two days just to get there. Somehow, she suspected this was more than a trip to Silver City.

"Where to, Papa?" Pansy asked.

"The ocean," replied Papa.

"The ocean! What ocean?" Pansy thought to herself. In the one room schoolhouse down the road, Pansy had learned about the United States. She knew very well there were no oceans anywhere near their log cabin ranch house in New Mexico. She knew on the east side of the United States was the Atlantic Ocean and on the west side was the Pacific Ocean. These oceans were hundreds of miles away and, by horse and wagon, would take months and months to reach.

Then, she remembered that the state next to them was Texas. Papa always talked about Texas and she had heard him say many times how he would like to see the land and people of that State. She also knew that on the southern border of Texas was another ocean.

"The Gulf of Mexico," Pansy spoke up suddenly.

"You are right!" said Papa with a smile.

"But that's so far away. How will we get there?" asked Pansy.

Papa began to explain how he had been planning this trip for some time.

When he was in Silver City, he bought some special supplies to take along with them and some lumber to make the wagon bigger.

He said, "We will need room to sleep and places to store things. I'll have to move Mama's stove up into the wagon, so she can cook while we travel. There are a lot of things to do, so we are going to be busy."

"When do we leave?" asked Pansy.

"As soon as things are ready," replied Papa.

Pansy asked, "How long will it take to get to the Gulf of Mexico?"

Papa said, "Pansy, it's over 800 miles from here to the Island of Galveston, Texas. We're not going to be in a hurry because there is so much to see along the way. It will take most of a year to go there and return to our home."

"A year!" exclaimed Pansy, "What about school, and who will take care of the ranch?"

"Slow down, Pansy," said Papa. "I've already thought about all of that and talked to your teacher. She is going to let you take along the books you would be learning from next year so you can study on the road."

"Oh . . ." Pansy sounded less than excited when she discovered there would still be school.

"Besides," said Papa, "this trip will be as good as any education for you."

For another hour, the family sat on the front porch of the log cabin ranch house and chatted about the plans for what now was being called the "Big Galveston Trip." As Pansy settled into bed that night, she could again hear the wind whistling through the prairie grass. This time, though, it was almost as if she could hear the sound of ocean waves while she slipped off to sleep.

Chapter 3

The Trip Begins

The dust from the wagon wheels rose like little puffs of clouds behind the wagon. Pansy had found a comfortable place, near the back, where she could lie on soft pillows and poke her head out of the canvas covering that stretched tight over the wagon. As they rode along the trail, she watched as the Capitan Mountains grew smaller and smaller in the distance. Tied to the back of the wagon were Jake and Willow, the two extra horses Papa brought along. Pansy could reach out the back of the wagon and just touch their noses, which they did not like, or offer them a carrot, which they did like.

Star was having fun running circles around the wagon. They were moving slowly. So slowly that Star could run off into the woods that lined the road and return before the wagon could travel very far. Pansy worried when Star disappeared into the woods, but Papa assured her saying, "That dog knows more about these woods than we do. He won't get lost. Besides, if you listen, you can hear him barking off in the distance even when you can't see him." Papa was right. Pansy could hear his screechy, high-pitched bark echoing from the woods. She laughed as she thought how his bark sounded less like a dog and more like a big bird. Only when Star sensed danger would he sound out with that low, rusty voice like the night the mountain lion had wandered near the ranch house.

The Trip Begins

The family had left the log cabin ranch house as the warm summer sun was rising over the mountains to the east. Pansy didn't know how far they had come, but they had been moving down the road at a steady pace for hours. After stopping by a chilly stream of water for lunch, they had pushed on and now the sun was beginning to settle down over the distant Capitan Mountains, which were growing smaller and smaller behind them. Papa had told the family he hoped to make fifteen or twenty miles each day, but they weren't in a hurry. There would be many things to stop and see along the way, and he intended for the family to be able to enjoy everything without feeling rushed.

About an hour before the sunset, Papa began looking for a place to camp for the night. The wagon was filled with supplies so Papa had built sideboards on the wagon, just the right size for each person to have a single mattress to sleep on. They also had a large tent for sleeping when there was rain. Papa had thought of everything. He even had moved Mama's stove into the wagon so she could cook. Under the wagon was a large cage for Mama's chickens. This meant they had fresh eggs every day. They were quite a sight coming down the road.

After many miles, Pansy had become use to the sounds of travel. It was like an orchestra. There was the clip-clop of horses' feet, the clucking of chickens, the rumble of the turning wheels on the road, the rattling of the supplies, and then the bark of Star circling the wagon. Clip-clop, rattle-rattle, cluck-cluck, rumble, rattle, roll, and bark-bark! "It is for sure, we aren't going to sneak up on anyone," Pansy laughed to herself.

Papa found a nice place along the road to camp for the night. Mama started dinner, and Papa gathered wood for a campfire. He then pulled chairs and a table out of the wagon. It would be just like dinner at home. Before long, they had eaten till they were full, then cleaned up the dishes with water from the stream nearby. As the last light disappeared over the mountains and the moon rose high in the sky, Papa lit the campfire and everyone sat around the blazing glow of orange and yellow light.

"Wonderful dinner, Mama," said Papa.

"Papa, will you tell us a story?" Pansy asked.

"Well . . . let me think," said Papa. "There is a story I've been saving for a long time and I think tonight may be the night to tell you. Unless you are too tired and want to go on to bed."

"No, no, I'm not tired at all, Papa," said Pansy.

Papa laughed along with Mama. "I thought that's what you would say. Well, okay."

Papa settled back in his chair with the soft glow of the campfire making his face take on a reddish shine. He stroked his beard and, as he began, Pansy could see his eyes brighten and flash. She had seen that look before. It always meant he was about to share something extra special.

He said, with a thoughtful voice, "This is the true story of your Great-Great Grandmother Nancy Ross."

Chapter 4

Great-Great Grandmother Stolen by Indians

Papa began the story. "When your Great-Great Grandmother Nancy Ross was just a young girl about your age, she lived in the State of Kentucky with her parents. They lived in a little log cabin, much like the one we live in, but instead of being at the base of a great mountain, it was nestled in the deep woods of Kentucky. This was a long time ago, just before the *United States became a Nation*. Nancy had long, dark black hair and dark brown eyes. I guess you could say she looked a lot like you, Pansy."

Papa went on, "Anyway, it was a time in our nation when there was war going on between the settlers and some of the Indian tribes. You see, Pansy, some of the settlers were building their houses and growing their crops on land that belonged to tribes of Indians for hundreds of years. In some places, the settlers and the Indians made agreements or *treaties* that permitted settlers to farm and build on the land, but in Kentucky, where Great-Great Grandmother Nancy Ross was living, there was no such treaty. In fact, the *Iroquois* Indian tribe had threatened to chase off the settlers and burn down their homes if they didn't leave."

Papa continued with an eager voice. "One day, while Nancy was in the yard feeding chickens and her mama was in the house washing clothes, they heard a loud shout and the sound of men yelling. Nancy looked up and saw her papa riding his horse, with the speed of lightning, across the field of corn he had planted. Right behind him, only a hundred yards away, was a band of Iroquois braves, chasing him on their horses, waving knives, tomahawks, and clubs."

"Nancy's papa rode into the yard, screaming, 'Get on your horses! Get on your horses and ride!'" Papa seemed almost breathless as he continued telling the story. "There was no time to saddle up. Nancy's mama jumped on the nearest horse in the corral, while Nancy climbed behind her and hung on for dear life. 'Go, Go, Go, Go, Go!!!' Yelled Nancy's father, and they left with the wind, just as the braves caught up with them. Some of the braves got off their horses and set fire to the log cabin."

Papa quickly continued, "Three of the Indians chased after your great-great grandmother and her parents. In those days, sometimes the Indians would steal a child from a settler's family to discourage other settlers from coming onto their land. Nancy's parents knew this and they rode like a flash to get away. The braves were very good at riding on horses with no saddle, but Nancy's mama had never ridden a horse bareback, so she wasn't able to ride nearly as fast."

"The braves were coming closer and closer. Nancy and her mama were riding faster and faster, but the braves were catching up. Nancy's papa saw what was happening and, courageously, turned his horse around to fight the braves. It was three against one and, while Papa was wrestling with one brave on his horse, a second brave struck him on the back of the head with a club, knocking him to the ground. The third brave kept riding until he caught up with Nancy and Mama. He reached out and plucked Nancy from the back of the horse. It was too easy and, in a flash, all three braves disappeared into the woods with the other warriors and Nancy."

The Indian Raid

Papa stopped to catch his breath, then continued the story. "The house was burning and Nancy was gone. Nancy's mama came back to find her husband thrown from his horse and sitting helplessly on the ground. There was no point in chasing the braves. They knew the woods too well and could have gone off in any direction. Nancy's papa and mama just sat there and cried. In a few moments, they had lost everything in the world that meant something to them. 'Nancy, Nancy!' her mama cried. Right then and there, Nancy's papa said to her mama, 'We must pray for her. We have to trust God to keep her safe and return her to us.' As Nancy's papa held onto her mama, they cried out to God to be with their little girl wherever she was taken."

Papa sadly continued the story, "Meanwhile, the braves returned to their tribe with the news they had chased out the settlers and stolen their child. Many of the tribe members celebrated at this success with hoops and yelling, cheering, and dancing. But, there was one member of the tribe who was not celebrating. Her name was *Lolotea*."

"Lolotea was an old Indian mother who had lived many years and was considered wise among the other women of the tribe. She had raised many children and the thought of some family losing their daughter, even if they were white settlers, was horrible to her. She kept silent but, in her heart, she planned to help this little girl the braves had stolen," said Papa.

"You see, sometimes God keeps us from trouble, and sometimes God keeps us safe in our trouble," Papa said slowly. "When Great-Great Grandmother Nancy was stolen by the Indians and her papa and mama knelt down to pray and cry out to God, He heard their prayers and touched the heart of Lolotea, who had a heart of love for children. This is what it means when the Bible says in Heb.13:5, (ESV), *'I will never leave you nor forsake you.'*"

Papa explained, "Nancy was frightened when the braves brought her into the camp, but she remembered the warning her father had taught her. He often said, 'If you are ever stolen by the Indians, do not show fear. Act brave and they will respect you, and let you live.' When the braves took Nancy off the horse and stood her in the middle of the big circle of Indians, they expected her to run. Nancy remembered what her father had told her and stood calmly, staring into the faces of her captors. The whole circle of braves grew silent, watching her stand tall, as she looked right back into their painted faces."

Papa continued to explain how courageous Nancy was before her captors. "One young brave yelled loudly at her in the language of the Iroquois. Nancy stood up, even taller, and looked him right in the eyes. The brave stopped yelling."

"Then, from behind the young braves, there stepped out a much larger Indian. He was older than the others and wore clothing and feathers that made him look, to Nancy, like he was perhaps the Chief or some important member of the tribe. When he stepped forward, all the braves moved aside to let him pass. He walked right up to your great-great grandmother and spoke something in the Iroquois language. Nancy didn't know what the Chief was saying, but she did understand one word. It was a word she had heard settlers use when they talked about others who had been captured by the Indians. The word was *gauntlet*!"

Papa continued with a description, "The gauntlet was when two rows of Indian braves stood facing each other, in a long line, about six or eight feet apart. Each brave would hold, in his hand, a club or knife of some kind. A captured settler would be forced to run from one end of the gauntlet to the other end. If they succeeded in running the whole length of the gauntlet, without being killed by the knives and clubs, the settler would be allowed to live among them. What Nancy remembered most from those stories was that almost no one survived the gauntlet. She tried to remain bold on the outside but, inside, she was trembling. Then, she felt a hand on her shoulder. This startled her more than the brave who yelled at her."

Papa quietly continued. "Nancy turned to look and saw Lolotea. She was surprised when the Indian woman spoke to her in English. 'Come with me,' she said. Lolotea took Nancy to her house. The Iroquois did not live in tents the way the Indians who lived on the plains are always shown in pictures. They lived in wooden *longhouse* structures deep in the woods and forests. Once in the house, Lolotea explained to Nancy that the next morning she would be made to run the gauntlet against young boys about her age. She warned they would be trying to hit her with clubs or even knives. She further explained they would want to kill her because there is great honor for the young brave who strikes a deadly blow."

Papa went on with the story. "Then, Lolotea told Nancy, 'I will explain to you how you can survive. You will put your hands on top of your head and lock your fingers together. When you start, run as fast as you can and don't stop, no matter what happens, or how hard you may be hit. Even if you are in pain, keep running. I will be sitting at the end of the gauntlet where you can see me. Don't take your eyes off me. Keep your hands over your head and keep on running until you run into my arms.'"

Papa continued, "Nancy wondered why the old woman was helping her, but she didn't question her instructions. Nancy wanted to get it over with. She did not want to wait all night but wished it could all be over right now. As the sun set in the sky, Nancy was given a meal of some kind of meat, probably *venison*. The old lady told her she had to eat to have strength to run the next morning. Nancy lay down, for the night, on a mattress of straw in the corner of the longhouse. She felt warm tears, as she thought about Papa and Mama, and how they must be very worried. She felt scared thinking about the morning and what would await her."

"It was then, that Nancy remembered the prayer she heard when the *circuit-riding preacher* would come to their settlement. It was from the Bible and Mama had taught her to say it by heart, *The Lord's Prayer*. She prayed it to God, as she lay on the bed of straw. 'Our Father, which art in heaven, hallowed be thy name. Thy kingdom come, thy will be done, on earth as it is in heaven. Give us this day our daily bread, and forgive us our trespasses as we forgive those who trespass against us. Lead us not into temptation but deliver us from evil. For thine is the kingdom, the power and the glory forever. Amen.' Then, she added. 'Lord, please help Papa and Mama to know that I'll be all right . . . and help me to be all right tomorrow, no matter what happens. Amen.'"

Papa paused, and then continued with the story. "Morning came too quickly for Nancy. The old woman shook her, got her up, and gave her something hot to drink. Nancy didn't know what it was, but it tasted awful. Lolotea insisted she drink all of it. Nancy could hear the tribe outside the old woman's door, whooping and yelling. They were chanting something that Nancy didn't understand. Lolotea led Nancy out the door and there she could see a long line of boys holding clubs and knives. Nancy's heart was beating fast as Lolotea led her to the starting line, and turned to say, 'When they tell you to go, don't wait. The faster you run, the better off you will be. I will be sitting at the end of the gauntlet where you can see me. Remember, don't take your eyes off me.'

Lolotea left Nancy with an older brave and made her way to the end of the line. Nancy could see the Chief standing with his arms crossed in the distance. It was only, then, that she noticed the large crowd that had assembled. There must have been two hundred spectators standing to watch the little white girl run the gauntlet. Everyone was cheering. She looked ahead and saw boy after boy with weapons, wielding above their heads, ready to strike. Every boy's eye was trained on Nancy. Then, she saw Lolotea sitting in a chair, at the end of the line, with her arms outstretched."

Papa quickly continued, "Nancy heard the brave next to her yell into her ear. She didn't wait but moved as fast as her legs could fly. She was aware that the first few braves missed, because they did not time their swing right, but then she felt the first thud on her back. She wanted to reach back with her hand and grab where it hurt, but she remembered the old woman said, 'Keep your hands locked onto your head.'

A bigger boy, with a club, hit her directly on top of her head, smashing her fingers, but she kept on running and running. Another boy hit her leg with his club, hoping to make her fall. She stumbled, but kept on going. One after another, some of the blows and cuts were so painful."

"Just as she felt she was slowing down, she heard the old Indian woman yelling, 'Keep running! Keep running!' In the middle of all this chaos, she remembered how only a day ago, it was her father telling her to run from the Indians. Then, she saw a shining knife blade stretched out in front of her. She felt it sliding across her forehead. How she made it on from there, she could only say 'was with God's help.' A moment later, she was in the arms of Lolotea."

Papa quickly concluded the story. "Nancy looked down and saw the old woman's dress was soaked in blood, her blood. She heard the shouts and screams of the tribe, but she didn't realize, at the time, they were now cheering for her. She had successfully run the gauntlet and would, forever, be considered a very special person in the tribe. Lolotea picked up Nancy's aching body and took her back to the longhouse to bandage her wounds."

Running the Gauntlet

Pansy listened in amazement as Papa told how Nancy's wounds slowly healed and about her life, being raised by the Indian tribe, in the home of Lolotea for the next seven years.

"Did she ever get back home?" wondered Pansy.

"Yes, but that's another story, for another night. Right now, it's bedtime," said Papa.

"Oh no, not now, Papa. Please tell me the rest of the story," begged Pansy.

Papa said to Pansy, "It's enough for you to know she eventually returns home, and she will be okay."

Pansy didn't argue with Papa anymore, as she knew he meant what he said. After saying her prayers, Pansy kissed Papa and Mama good night. As she was crawling up onto her bed that was hooked onto the side of the wagon, she turned around to Papa and said, "Papa?"

"Yes, Pansy."

"Could that still happen? I mean, could Indians still capture girls like me?"

"No, Pansy. Those wars are all over and these days we live in peace with the Indians."

"Whew!" Pansy sighed. "I am sure glad to hear that!"

Papa and Mama laughed with her. Pansy lay in bed looking straight up at the summer stars twinkling above her. She thought to herself how glad she was that Papa had decided to take this trip. She wondered how many more stories, like the one she had heard tonight, would lie ahead.

Chapter 5

Lolotea and The Horse Soldiers

Two days passed and Pansy was still thinking about the story Papa had told her of Great-Great Grandmother Nancy. As Pansy walked along beside the moving wagon, Star stayed close by her side. Somehow, Star always knew when Pansy was troubled or worried. In those times, he would stay close to her side, wagging his stubby black tail like a whip, and looking up at her from time to time. Pansy looked down at Star. She seemed to know he was worried about her.

"It's okay, boy," said Pansy, "I'm just thinking about things." She picked up a fallen stick, which had broken off a sycamore tree hanging over the road.

"Get it, boy," said Pansy, and then sent the stick sailing past the team of horses. Star scrambled to the stick moments after it landed.

"Pansy!" yelled Papa from the wagon seat. "You are going to scare these horses by throwing sticks in front of them." Pansy knew he was right.

"Sorry, Papa!" Pansy responded. Meanwhile, Star came running back, with the stick in his mouth, ready for another round.

Pansy was just about to throw the stick again only, this time, in another direction, when Mama's voice spoke up, from the back of the wagon.

29

"Pansy?" Mama called. "Who were you talking to a minute ago?"

"Oh," Pansy smiled. "I was talking to Star."

"I see," said Mama. "Do you talk to Star often?" Mama asked, with a chuckle in her voice.

"Only when I feel kind of bad," Pansy replied.

"Why do you feel bad?" Mama asked. Pansy began telling Mama how she keeps thinking about what it must have been like to be captured by Indians and kept from family for so long.

"It was a good thing Lolotea was there to care for my great-great grandmother or she might not have survived," said Pansy in a happier tone.

"That's, almost, for certain," said Mama, as she climbed down out of the wagon and began to walk beside Pansy. "In fact, Lolotea saved Nancy's life twice."

"Really?" questioned Pansy. "Did she have to run the gauntlet again?"

"Oh, no," said Mama. "After she ran the gauntlet once, she was considered a princess and was respected by the tribe. Although, they wouldn't let her go home, they took special care of her. They gave her food, water, and made sure she was protected. In winter, she was given a warm blanket to sleep under, and she was always given plenty to eat."

Mama continued, "For a short time, things were all right for Nancy, but then one day the *horse soldiers* came to the camp."

"Who are they?" asked Pansy.

"Well, in those days, the army had horse soldiers. They are soldiers who are trained to ride and fight from their horses. These soldiers were looking for the Indians that had been killing settlers and burning their houses to the ground. The tribe of Indians, where Great-Great Grandmother Nancy lived learned that the soldiers were nearby, so they moved all of the women and children into a secret canyon up in the hills to protect them. Of course, Lolotea and Nancy went into hiding along with the rest of the tribe."

Lolotea

"Well," Mama went on, "A horse soldier accidentally discovered where the Indian women and children were hidden. The captain of the horse soldiers was a man by the name of Cook."

"Really?" Asked Pansy.

"Yes," Mama replied. "Captain Cook, just like the famous English Naval Captain who traveled around the world, but this Captain was not a good man. He was mean and hated Indians."

"So, what happened?" wondered Pansy.

Mama explained the story. "When Captain Cook found the defenseless women and children hidden in the canyon, he told his men to ride into the camp and start slashing them with their swords. Many of the horse soldiers following Captain Cook knew this was not right for armed soldiers to hurt or kill innocent women and children. When they rode into the camp, they swung their swords, yelling and hollering, but they intentionally missed the Indian women and children, allowing them to run away into the forest. They refused to dishonor themselves by hurting innocent people.

Captain Cook, on the other hand, was a bloodthirsty fighter and wanted to cause pain and suffering, especially to the Indians. He rode into the camp, yelling at the top of his lungs and wildly swinging his sword. He saw an old woman and a young girl hiding behind a tree. It was Lolotea and your Great-Great Grandmother Nancy Ross. Of course, Nancy looked and was dressed just like all the other Indian children. When Lolotea saw the Captain coming after them, she grabbed Nancy and they ran.

"Remember, Pansy, we told you that Nancy had black hair, dark skin, and looked much like an Indian?" Mama asked.

"Yes," said Pansy, "I remember."

Of course, they were no match for the speed of Captain Cook's horse and he quickly had them pinned up against another tree. As he lifted his sword, Lolotea instinctively grabbed Nancy and covered her head with her hands to protect her. The Captain's mighty sword came down right on top of Lolotea's hands and Nancy's head. The sword sliced through some of Lolotea's fingers, then cut a gash in the top of Nancy's skull. The wound was bad, but one that would heal. The Captain laughed and rode off, cursing and chasing another Indian woman, while Nancy and Lolotea stood in shock at what had just happened.

The old woman's first concern was not the loss of her fingers. In fact, years later, Nancy would tell her family that she never saw Lolotea cry or express pain over what happened. She immediately began to pour water on Nancy's head and she found a cloth to cover Nancy's wounded scalp. It was only after she was sure Nancy would be okay that she began to tend to her own injuries."

"Lolotea was a wonderful woman," said Pansy.

"You're right, Pansy. We can all learn from this story that there are good and bad people of all races and colors. There were bad Indians that killed and burned the homes of innocent white people, but there were also bad soldiers, like Captain Cook, who would attack innocent Indian women and children. On the other hand, there were beautiful and gracious Indians, like Lolotea, who protected and loved Nancy. Also, there were the honorable and brave horse soldiers, who refused to follow the angry Captain's order to kill innocent people. In other words, Pansy, there are good and bad people everywhere of all differing races and beliefs."

"Mama, that is a wonderful story," Pansy said.

"Oh Pansy, that's not the end of the story."

"It's not?" Pansy asked.

Mama began the story again, "No, no! Many years later after your great-great grandmother was returned to her family, had married, and was now a beautiful young woman, she and her husband were invited to a very elegant dinner with many important people. Everyone was dressed in fancy clothes. It was a very special affair. As the guests arrived at the party, there was a servant by the door who would loudly announce the name of each guest, welcoming them to the gathering. Nancy and her husband were visiting with the other friends when, all at once, she heard the name being announced, 'Please welcome the honorable Captain Cook!' She turned to see the face of the man who had cut Lolotea's fingers off and deeply scarred her own head.

Nancy wanted to be polite and, at first, said nothing to anyone, but the Captain was a preposterous, loud, and boastful man. She could hear his booming voice bragging to some of the other men about the great battles he had fought. In the course of his bragging, he began to talk about the time he and his horse soldiers had attacked a village of Indian women and children. He was laughing as he talked about cutting the fingers of an old Indian woman and the head of her dirty little child.

At that, your beautiful Great-Great Grandmother Nancy stepped into the circle of men, looked straight into the Captain's eyes and said to him, as she lowered her head and parted her hair, 'Do you see that scar on my head, honorable Captain?' The Captain was startled and said nothing. Nancy lifted her head, looked straight into his eyes, and said, 'Captain, I was that dirty little child you cut with your sword. That horrible old Indian woman, as you called her, sacrificed her fingers to save my life. She is my hero and, you may be a Captain, but you are anything but honorable.' Silence filled the room. The Captain was very pale, never said a word, but turned and quickly left the party in shame."

Mama continued, "Of course, everyone at the party knew the story of your great-great grandmother's capture by the Indians, but now they understood and respected her even more as they realized, not only had she been captured and tortured by the Indians, but also by this captain as well. They respected her for standing up to him and defending Lolotea."

Nancy and Captain Cook

Pansy thought for a moment, and then said, "Mama, Great-Great Grandmother Nancy Ross was a strong and special person."

Mama smiled at Pansy and said, "That strength came from trusting God in the trials she went through. The Bible calls people like your grandmother *overcomers*. These are special people who have learned to trust God in every situation."

"Pansy, that same strength is in you! You just have to look for it and use it. The same God that was in her life is also in yours. In time, you can be a woman of God just like your Great-Great Grandmother Nancy."

Pansy had to think about that.

Chapter 6

The Rescue

Rumble, Rumble, Crash!!! The day began with a flash of lightning and the rumble of thunder. Pansy poked her head out from under the covers to see that the morning sky was almost as dark as Star's black face. With each crash of thunder, the chickens would cackle wildly and Star would howl.

Pansy could hear Papa and Mama on the other side of the wagon, rushing about to secure everything from the coming rainstorm. All the supplies had to be stored in the wagon, along with the mattresses. Pansy jumped from her perch and began picking up everything she could. One thing you learned, living with Papa and Mama Hunt, was that everyone had to do their part to help. Pansy didn't wait to be asked or told to help. She knew she was expected to pitch in and help and she did.

In a few minutes, everything was loaded and, as Papa hitched up the team of horses, the first sprinkles of rain began to fall. "Yah!" Hollered Papa to the horses pulling the wagon and they began to move ahead. Mama and Pansy were dry and comfortable inside the covered wagon, but poor Papa had to sit outside and guide the horses as the sprinkles turned into a downpour.

The mountains were not a safe place to be in a bad storm, and this one looked like it would be pretty rough. Papa knew there was a town only a few miles ahead in the valley that stretched out below the mountain range. For an hour, the horses pulled the wagon along the dirt road until the dirt turned into mud. Even in mud, the horses could still pull the wagon but not as fast.

Star had found refuge inside the wagon up next to the cooking stove. Pansy smiled as she thought how often Star would curl up on the old Indian rug in front of the sink at home. To Star, this probably felt like a safe and familiar spot. Mama and Pansy sat on big cushions they had brought along for the ride. The bump, bump, bumps had turned to splash, splash, splashes!

"Mama, "Whatever happened to my Great-Great Grandma Nancy?" Pansy asked. "Papa said she finally got back home, but how?"

"I don't suppose Papa would mind if I told you the rest of the story," said Mama, "Especially, since we're going to be cooped up in this wagon for awhile."

"Well, Pansy, your Great-Great Grandmother Nancy Ross recovered from all her wounds with the help of Lolotea, her Indian mother. After successfully running the gauntlet, Nancy was accepted and respected by the tribe. In fact, she was treated like a princess. They gave her the best of everything, but they would not let her return home."

Pansy asked, "How long did she live with the Indians?"

Mama said, "For seven years."

"Wow! That's a long time!" said Pansy.

"Yes, and her Papa and Mama never stopped looking for her. They hired *Scouts* to hunt for her."

"What's a Scout, Mama?" asked Pansy.

"Well, Pansy, a Scout is an Indian who works for the army. They know the customs and ways of the Indians and they helped the army work out some of the troubles between the Indians and settlers," answered Mama.

She continued, "For many months, an Indian Scout had been looking for a young, white woman in all of the tribes around the area."

"Wait, Mama. You said Nancy was only seven or eight years old."

"I know, but it had been seven years since she was stolen, so now she was fourteen, almost fifteen years old, and a young lady," said Mama.

"So, how did he find her?" Pansy asked.

Mama replied, "It wasn't easy. Your great-great grandmother was so dark skinned with black hair, that she actually looked like she could be an Indian. The Scout had heard stories of a white woman, in a certain tribe, who had successfully run the gauntlet about the time Nancy had been stolen, so he went to the tribe to check on it.

He couldn't just walk in and ask if she was there because that would raise too much suspicion. He came to the tribe, saying he was from another friendly tribe, and wanted to trade for animal skins. That way, no one would suspect why he was really there. While visiting, he kept a lookout for the young, white girl. He stayed for three days talking to the Chief and the other braves about deerskins. He was about to give up and leave when he spotted a young girl about the right age. She was wearing the clothing of the Indian tribe but she, somehow, looked a little different in the face. He watched her walking through the camp, but not so closely that he would draw too much attention.

He went back inside the Chief's longhouse and told him he had decided to make a trade with the tribe and would be staying a couple more days. The Chief was pleased and invited him to stay in his longhouse for the night. The Scout knew if he did that, it would be very hard for him to slip away and learn what he needed to know about this young girl. He thanked the Chief, but asked if he might stay outside the camp near his own supplies. The Chief agreed and asked him to come again in the morning."

Mama continued, "It was a daily routine for the young girls of the tribe to rise early in the morning to go down to the stream to fetch water for the day. The Scout planned to be at the stream early in the morning, with his horse, so it looked like he was just watering his horse when, in fact, he was really watching for the young girl. Shortly after the sun rose, the Scout was already at the stream where the girls fetched water. One or two at a time, they came to the water's edge and dipped their buckets into the stream, and then returned home.

After a few minutes, he spotted her. Fortunately, she was alone. As she came near the water, the Scout stepped out and asked if her name was Nancy, and if she was a white girl who had been captured seven years ago.

Nancy looked around, nervously, and said, 'Yes, who are you?'

He told her he was a Scout and had been looking for her many months. He knew if he stayed too long and talked to her, someone would notice, and there might be suspicion concerning why he was really there. He quickly said to her, 'Be here tomorrow morning right after the sun rises. I'll have two horses and will take you back to your family.'

'How are they?' Nancy asked, hoping they were all right.

The Scout answered, 'They have been searching for you many years. I want to get you back to them as fast as possible.' For seven years, she wondered if the Indians had killed her parents after taking her away. She was relieved to learn that they were both alive and well."

Mama continued, "Quickly, Nancy returned to her house so no one would suspect anything was wrong. Although the Indians treated her like a princess, they never allowed her the freedom to leave the area or even roam about on her own.

As Nancy walked back up the hill toward her longhouse, she thought of seeing her parents again. She also thought of Lolotea. This will break her heart. For seven years, she had cared for and loved Nancy like a mother. She had risked the anger of the tribe by helping Nancy run the gauntlet, and she raised Nancy like her own daughter. Now, she had to leave her without even being able to say goodbye."

Mama quickly said, "Before she went to bed that night, she found the old Indian woman busy sewing and repairing some clothing near the fireplace. She went up to Lolotea, put her arms around her neck, and told her thank you for always being so good to her.

'I love you, Lolotea,' Nancy said. Lolotea put down her sewing and held Nancy by the cheeks, looking into her eyes.

'Are you all right?' Lolotea asked.

'Yes,' Nancy said.

'I love you, too, child,' and she kissed her on the forehead.

Nancy looked down at the few remaining fingers on Lolotea's hands. They had been sacrificed to save her life. She was amazed that, with only half of her fingers, she was still able to sew. Never once had she heard Lolotea complain. Nancy thought to herself how much this Indian mother loved her and how painful it would be to leave her.

Nancy went to bed and nothing more was said between them. She would always think that Lolotea probably knew something was about to happen to take her away, but she did nothing to prevent it. It was her way to love and want the very best for others. Her name, Lolotea, means, "gift from God" and, for your great-great grandmother, she truly was a very special gift."

Pansy agreed, "Mama, she was a wonderful mother."

"Yes, she was, Pansy," Mama answered, as she continued with excitement in her voice, "The next morning very early, as the sun was just rising, Nancy met the Scout at the stream outside the camp. In a moment, they rushed away on the horses. There was no time to waste. As soon as others realized she was gone, they would send braves out on horses to find her.

Nancy and Lolotea

Away they rode like a flash. It was about two miles from the Indian camp to the *blockhouse* where the soldiers lived. The Scout had prepared the troops and they were watching from the top of the blockhouse with guns, ready to shoot, if any braves were chasing them or getting too close.

Sure enough, not long after they left the camp of the Indians, someone saw them riding away, and the warning was echoed all over the camp. Young braves rode fast after them. Fortunately, they had only bows and arrows, but no guns, so by the time they almost caught up, the two of them were safely inside the blockhouse. The Indians knew not to come too close to the blockhouse because the soldiers had powerful guns, so they returned to their camp."

Mama said light-heartedly, "Pansy, that is how your great-great grandmother was rescued and returned to her parents. Nancy Ross lived to be one hundred years old and had a great grandson, named John Ross, who became a well-known evangelist. He wrote a book about her and that's how we know the story of her capture and rescue."

After Mama finished the story, Pansy just sat for a while and thought about her Great-Great Grandmother Nancy Ross. She hardly noticed when Star left his post near the stove and curled up near her feet. For a long time, she sat quietly looking out the back of the wagon. She was aware of the rainstorm and thunder, but her thoughts were on how hard it must have been for little Nancy to be separated from her papa and mama for so many years, never knowing if she would ever see them again. She also thought about how God kept His promise to never leave or forsake her. Even though it took seven years, God brought her safely home.

Chapter 7

Snakes

The short trip that rainy day had actually taken hours. Papa knew there was a town just down in the valley below the mountain. What he didn't know was that they would have to cross a flooded stream of water nineteen times to get to the town. Most of the stream crossings were shallow, but some of them were deep and treacherous. The horses would pull the wagon down into the stream then, with their great strength; they would fight against the rapids coming swiftly down the mountain until the wagon was safely on the other side.

One time, the water was half way up the wagon wheels, which meant it was almost in the wagon. The chickens were all in their cages under the wagon, which meant they were under water, and Pansy was frightened they would drown. As the horses fought against the powerful surge of water and pulled the wagon up again out of the stream, Pansy could hear the chickens wildly cackling below the floor of the wagon and she knew they were okay. It was probably the scariest day of the trip until they came to the city of San Antonio, Texas.

Papa had talked about visiting San Antonio for years. He had a lot of knowledge about the history of the city from reading books. The place he most wanted his family to see was the *Alamo* where, in the year 1836, over two hundred Texans lost their lives in a battle against the Mexican army led by General Santa Anna.

Today, the Alamo is a museum and a national memorial where thousands of people visit each year. When Papa and Mama Hunt took Pansy to visit the Alamo, the memories of the lives lost there were still very fresh and many of the families who lost loved ones there were still living and considered the site a sacred place.

Even though the Texas army lost the battle at the Alamo, it was the memory of that loss which caused future soldiers to shout, "Remember the Alamo!" as they defeated Santa Anna and his Mexican army in the battle at San Jacinto a few weeks later. "This is how Texas won its independence," said Papa, "and, later, became one of the states in the United States of America." Well, Papa could go on and on talking about the great State of Texas and the heroes of the Alamo like Davy Crockett and Daniel Boone.

They were sitting around the campfire, just outside San Antonio, as Papa was explaining the coming day and their anticipated ride into the city. Papa was so caught up in his story that he hardly noticed how Star was growling low under his breath with his face pointed directly at the rock Pansy was sitting on.

"What's that dog doing?" Mama asked, interrupting Papa's tale.

Pansy looked into Star's eyes, and then followed his stare to a place just behind her. There coiled up like a neatly rolled-up rope was a snake. A RATTLE SNAKE!!! The snake wasn't paying any attention to Pansy because it was focused on Star and his growl. They had locked eyes on each other and neither one wanted to make the next move.

Papa picked up a smooth rock and told Pansy, "When I throw this rock, you run to me. Ready, one…two…three!"

He threw the rock, which missed the snake, but distracted it for a moment, while Pansy moved like a flash toward her father. Mama sat with her hands over her mouth and Star used the moment to begin his low, rusty bark. The snake, which was more frightened than anyone in the camp, turned and slithered away.

45

Star and the Rattlesnake

Papa grabbed his oil lantern and lifted it up to give more light to the circle they were sitting in. One two, three, four…five snakes! There were snakes all over the place! They had camped in a very bad spot. Nobody slept very well that night. Pansy had visions of snakes crawling into her bed, which Papa said was impossible. Everyone was worried about the horses and chickens, but they knew Star would be on the watch for trouble.

A couple times in the night, Star growled, which woke up everyone. Pansy dreamed about snakes in her bed but, thankfully, the sun came up and Papa hitched up the team of horses and they headed on to San Antonio. This morning they skipped breakfast because nobody wanted to be in that spot one minute longer than they had to stay. Mama and Pansy were glad to feel the tug of the wagon and the turning of the wheels as they left that campsite.

"Wow!" Pansy exclaimed. "I'm glad that is over!"

"Not quite," hollered Papa from the seat of the wagon. "Come up here and look." Mama and Pansy poked their heads out of the front opening to the wagon where Papa was sitting. Ahead of them on the road and all along the ditches, on either side, Papa was pointing out snakes.

"This is rattlesnake country," said Papa.

The noise and clanging of the wagon going down the road was scaring the snakes from their hiding places under rocks. Some were crossing the road and others were slithering off into the tall grass along the side.

"I'm never getting out of this wagon again," said Pansy.

"I don't blame you," replied Papa "but we'll soon be out of here and away from the snakes." Papa had to admit that he, too, was a little worried and anxious to get on into San Antonio.

When they arrived in the city, they told people they met about their adventure. Most locals just laughed and said, "The snakes were here first. They own this city. They are everywhere!"

Despite this, Papa was anxious to press on to the middle of the town and see the Alamo. Down dusty streets they rolled along, sounding like a noisy out-of-tune band, clanging here and squeaking there. Three sets of eyes were taking in the sights of the city. This was the first time Pansy had actually been in a town larger than a postage stamp. There were shops and cafés, tall buildings, and people bustling around everywhere. There were streetlights along the major avenues, something they didn't have back in Lincoln. It was all very new and fascinating to Pansy.

"There it is!" announced Papa happily.

"What?" Mama and Pansy asked in unison.

"Alamo Street," said Papa.

Papa led the horses to the right around the corner and began to make his way along the avenue called Alamo Street. Along the way, Pansy noticed they were attracting some attention with their unusual and noisy wagon. People would stop and look. Meanwhile, Papa would smile and wave to them.

One time, Papa hollered to a man standing near the street. Papa spoke in Spanish "Buena dia, esta es el camino a la Alamo?" Papa was asking if this was the way to the Alamo.

"Si, continuar." He told them to keep going.

Papa could speak Spanish pretty well because he lived among Spanish-speaking people much of his life and did business with them. Papa had ranch hands that spoke mostly Spanish, so he learned to talk with them. Papa sometimes would say, "You have to speak a man's language to know his heart." Pansy wasn't sure what that meant, but she often heard him say the phrase.

They pressed on down the streets a few more blocks when, all of a sudden; on their right was the Alamo. It looked like many Catholic Church missions Papa had seen before. White limestone blocks with arching doors and windows. It had a high steeple with an arched opening in the tower. As they pulled to a stop, they saw other visitors quietly walking around the area. Papa reminded Pansy that this was a very sacred place, almost like a cemetery, because so many brave men lost their lives right on this spot.

Climbing down from the wagon, they walked through the mission and around the grounds. There were artifacts on display from the battle and the names of more than two hundred soldiers, who lost their lives, were listed on the wall. Papa took time to sit with Mama and Pansy on a stone bench, close to the front door of the Alamo. For a few minutes, they just looked around. Papa then began to talk about what it means for a person to die for their country and for freedom.

Papa explained, "It means that the soldier is willing to trade all of his future days for the chance of giving freedom to others."

He continued, "This nation was paid for with the lives of such brave people. We can read and study about it but, when you sit here and imagine that just a few years ago real men with wives and families and dreams of their own were willing to sacrifice their dreams so we could enjoy ours, it is very amazing."

Pansy thought she saw tears welling up in Papa's eyes. He quickly wiped his forehand across his face and then stood up. A few feet away were two flagpoles, one flying the Texas flag, and the other flying the American flag. Papa took Mama and Pansy by the hand and together they walked over and stood under the flags. There, Papa bowed his head and prayed for the families of these and all soldiers who have given their lives for our freedom. They walked quietly back to the wagon, climbed in, and began to pull away. Pansy had rarely seen Papa so moved in his emotions.

After they had traveled a short way, Papa asked who was hungry. He had spotted a café, with a sign in front, which said they served the best Mexican food in San Antonio.

"Let's stop and eat here," said Papa. Mama looked at Papa as though he had lost his mind. Papa never ate at a café. Even when he was on the road traveling, he would always take supplies along to fix dinner over a campfire.

"You want to eat at a café?" Mama questioned, thinking she must have misunderstood.

"Sure!" Papa said, "The sign says it's the best Mexican food in San Antonio!"

Mama looked at Papa and, with a knowing smile, said to him, "Papa, every café we have passed in this city has a sign saying they are the best in San Antonio."

Papa laughed and began to pull the team to a stop. The three of them entered the café and enjoyed a wonderful meal. For Mama and Pansy, this was highly unusual. No cooking or cleaning up afterwards.

"I could get use to this!" Mama smiled, as she patted Papa on the back.

"Truth is, Mama, I don't want to camp anywhere near San Antonio and those snakes. Now, that we have had dinner, I can move on and put as many miles between those critters and me as possible. No campin' or cookin' tonight!" With that, Papa paid the waiter and the family headed east out of the city toward Galveston.

Chapter 8

Aunt Virginia

It was a beautiful summer night. The sun was just about to set over the vast Texas prairie. Dinner was finished, the dishes were washed, and everyone was sitting around the campfire as they so often did on this trip. Pansy could see this was going to be a story-telling night. She could always see the glimmer in Papa's eyes, as he was anxious for everyone to sit and visit. As the sun disappeared over the hills, the night air became chilly and the campfire felt warm, inviting them to move closer. Even in the summer, the nights could be chilly on the prairie.

"Tell us a story," Pansy said to Papa, not that she really thought he needed to be encouraged to do so. Papa was a storyteller and was always ready to spin a tale.

"Hmmm," said Papa. "Have I ever told you about your great *Aunt Virginia*?" Now Pansy's middle name was Virginia and she had often wondered why her parents had chosen that name.

"That's my middle name . . ." She knew it well. Whenever she would get in a little trouble, Mama would yell out the door, "Pansy Virginia . . . come in here right now!" For some reason, when a kid is in trouble, this is the only time parents use their middle name. This may have been why she was not very fond of the name.

"Let me tell you why your middle name is Virginia," said Papa. "You are named after my Aunt Virginia. She lived most of her life in the State of Kansas." Pansy knew that Kansas was a state just north of Texas and Oklahoma but she had never been there.

"What did she do?" asked Pansy.

"Well," Papa explained, "it's not so much any one thing she did, as it is the story of her whole life. You see, Pansy, Virginia was raised up in the Capitan Mountains the same as you. There, she met William Rule, the man who became her husband, and they moved to Kansas to farm and raise a family. Virginia was a very special woman because, in her lifetime, she faced many difficult and almost impossible situations, but she always trusted God to help her through them. She is what people call 'an inspiration to the rest of us.'"

"What kind of troubles did she have, Papa?" asked Pansy.

Before Papa could answer, Pansy said, "Do you mean like the trouble Great-Great Grandma Nancy faced when she was stolen by the Indians?"

"Well, Pansy," said Papa, "Aunt Virginia was never stolen by Indians, but she faced some really big troubles, and her life shows the rest of us that when you trust God, He will always be there to help you."

Papa sat back in his chair and rubbed his chin as he thought about where to begin his story. Pansy was sitting on the edge of her seat like a dry cactus flower ready to soak up the rain.

"Pansy," said Papa. "There are many stories I could tell but I think I'll begin with the fire."

"What fire?" Pansy said with excitement and anticipation.

Papa began the story. "Well, Aunt Virginia and her husband, William, moved to Kansas and found a little *farm* to buy. William bought the farm with money he had been saving for a long time. His whole life savings, every dime went into the purchase of that farm. Now, you have to understand that both Uncle William and Aunt Virginia loved God. They tried to honor God with everything they owned.

William would plow the ground, plant the seed, and work hard every day of the week. When Sunday came, he refused to do any work around the farm except feed the livestock because, of course, the animals needed to eat.

On Sunday, he and Virginia would put on proper Sunday clothes and attend the little country church, which was about two miles down the road from their house. William would hitch up the team of horses to the wagon. He and Virginia would sit up on the wagon seat and their two children, Ernest and John, would ride in the back. Together, they would go to church every Sunday, no matter what. If it was raining or snowing, it didn't matter, because they were faithful people who loved God."

Papa quickly continued, "One Sunday, as they were sitting in church, right during the middle of the preacher's sermon, a man crashed through the doors of the sanctuary and screamed, 'There's a fire down the road!!! Someone's house is on fire!!!' Indeed, it was. When they looked out the side windows of the church, everyone could see black smoke billowing up into the hot morning sky. William and Virginia knew immediately that it was their house. They also knew, by the amount of smoke and how long it would take to get there that there was little hope of saving anything. They were right.

Everyone in the church jumped in their wagons and on their horses to race to the fire, but by the time they arrived, most of the house was reduced to charred burning embers laying on the ground. It was a total loss. The fire destroyed everything they owned. Every bit of clothing, furniture, pictures, and keepsakes were burned. All of Virginia's dishes, pots, and pans were mostly melted in the heat. Even some money William kept in a safe place under the bed was gone. As neighbors gathered around them, William and Virginia, with their two boys, huddled together in the front yard where their house once stood. They didn't complain. They didn't get mad at God. They didn't even ask for help from the neighbors.

They got down on their knees right there in front of that disaster and prayed to God. They said, 'Lord, everything we have is yours and we have always trusted you to take care of us. Please take care of us now in whatever way that pleases you. We trust you, Lord! Amen.'"

Papa said, "All that was left, when the fire was over, was the *foundation*."

"What's a foundation?" Pansy asked.

Papa answered, "Well, that's actually the most important part of the house because it's the concrete part on which the house is built. William cleared away all the burnt wood and measured the foundation because he was planning to build a new house on top of that old concrete foundation. He measured and discovered the foundation to be fifty feet wide and sixty-five feet long."

Papa said, "Remember those numbers, Pansy, because it's important!"

Papa continued the story, "William wrote down those numbers on a piece of paper and, on Monday, headed toward town to price the lumber needed to build a new house. Of course, William didn't have enough money to buy the lumber. He had spent all he had to buy the land and house that burnt down."

Papa explained, "William planned to go to the bank and ask if he could borrow the money for the lumber. However, before he left home, both he and Virginia prayed and asked for the favor of God. When he got to town, William priced the lumber, and then went to the bank to ask about borrowing the money.

He sat down with Mr. Schultz, the banker, who told William how sad he was that they had lost their house. He said he would be glad to loan them the money but, before he did that, he asked William if he would be interested in a brand new house that a friend of his in another town wanted to sell. Mr. Schultz told William that the house would have to be moved, but it was a good house, and had never been lived in."

The House Fire

Papa continued, "Well, of course, William was interested, so he returned home to tell Pansy and, again, they prayed for God's help. The next day, William left to go see the mysterious, brand new house that was for sale. He met the owner and, together, they rode out to the edge of town where he saw a very beautiful, brand new home.

William took one look at the house and wondered why this man would want to sell such a nice house right after it had been built. He asked the man why he wanted to sell the house. He began to cry. The man explained that he had built the house for his son as a wedding gift. A week before he was to be married, his son was killed in an accident on the farm. The man wiped the tears from his eyes. I don't even want to see this house here anymore. I was told you lost everything in a fire. You can have this house if you will move it from this spot to your own property."

Papa said, "William could hardly believe his ears. He put his arm around the old man's shoulders and thought about how blessed he was to have only lost a home and some household things, while this man had lost the son he loved so much. He told him how sorry he was that he had lost his son and the man said, 'If you want the house, please just take it. I'm giving it to you, just like I planned to give it to my own son.'"

"Now, Pansy, do you remember when we were talking about the size of the foundation?" asked Papa.

Pansy replied, "Yes, Papa. It was fifty feet wide and sixty-five feet long."

"Good job remembering, Pansy," said Papa. He then continued with the story.

"William looked at the house. He looked at the old man. He then took out his tape measure and walked over to the front of the house and stretched out the line and measured the width of the house. It measured exactly fifty feet wide. He reset the tape and measured the length of the house. It measured exactly sixty-five feet long. This house was exactly the same size as the foundation back on the farm.

Now, William had tears in his own eyes, as he realized that God had provided exactly what they needed and more. God had provided a house that fit exactly on the foundation of his burned down farmhouse. It was as though God was saying to William, 'My son, I will never leave you or forsake you. Just trust me.'"

Pansy thought about the story Papa had just told for a long time, as she stared deep into the glowing campfire. "I have a question, Papa," she said. "It's wonderful that our Aunt Virginia and Uncle William got that house but…"

"But what?" questioned Papa with a knowing glance.

"Why did that nice man's son have to die?" asked Pansy.

"Oh, Pansy, there are many things in life we don't understand. Part of trusting God is learning that we won't always have all the answers to our questions," said Papa.

Pansy thought, then asked, "But, did God make him die?"

"I don't think so, Pansy," said Papa. "I don't think it was ever God's plan for people to die, get sick, or experience pain and sorrow, but we know in this life these things do happen. What God does is take the bad things that go wrong and bring good from them."

"You mean the way this man's sorrow ended up helping someone else?" asked Pansy.

"That's right!" said Papa. "We know how the story ended with your Aunt Virginia. I like to think, in some way, God also brought about something good for the old man who gave his house to William."

"I guess it's a real good thing to always trust God," said Pansy.

Mama, who hadn't said a word all night, spoke up, "Pansy, that reminds me of a scripture in the Bible which says, 'Trust in the LORD with all your heart; and do not lean on your own understanding. In all your ways acknowledge him, and He will make straight your paths.'" (Prov. 3:5-6, ESV)

"That's right, Mama," said Papa.

"Pansy, can you see how, even though Uncle William and Aunt Virginia went through a really bad experience, God used their trouble to show them how much He loved and would take care of them?"

"I sure do!" exclaimed Pansy.

That night as Pansy crawled on her bed and looked up into the starry sky above, she was thinking about her aunt and how really glad she was that her middle name was Virginia.

Chapter 9

A New Friend

The morning sun was peaking over the tall pine trees to the east of the camp when Papa's voice invaded Pansy's sleep.

"Pansy!" Papa's voice rang in her ears. "It's late and we have a big day ahead," he said in his no nonsense time-to-get-out-of-bed voice.

With one eye open and the other still nearly shut, Pansy shuffled off her bunk and down to the ground below. She heard the cackling of the chickens, as Mama looked for fresh eggs in their cages, under the wagon. She could hear Star barking, as he raced in circles around what was left of the smoking campfire. The smell of fresh pine needles and fall sweet weeds filled her head.

Pansy stood on the ground and thought, "What a wonderful idea Papa had coming on this trip. Even with the flooded streams and the snakes, it has been a great adventure." Pansy liked adventure. Every day she was seeing something new she had never seen before, and experiencing places and people that were interesting and wonderful. "Who knows what the road ahead will bring today," she thought to herself.

For four months, they had traveled all the way from their log cabin ranch in New Mexico across miles and miles of Texas prairie and badlands filled with cactus and rocks, on their way to the Island of

Galveston. Sometimes, Papa would stop and spend a few days in a pretty spot just to enjoy the view. True to his word, Papa was not in a hurry. They traveled when they wanted and rested when they wanted.

Last night they had camped in a *community campground* outside one of the many small towns they had come through. They were not the only travelers on the road. In fact, the longer they journeyed, the more they encountered other people who also were moving about from city to city. Many of the small towns had campgrounds on the edge of the city where people who were passing through could stop for the night. The campgrounds had special places for the horses, and shelters to protect people from the weather while they were eating. Some of them even had places to take a hot bath. It was almost like being home.

The best part of the community campground, for Pansy, was the other children. Growing up on the prairie was wonderful, but she didn't get a lot of opportunity to play with other children, except at school. At the campgrounds, there were often many other children who also were traveling with their parents. Some of them were on long trips, like Pansy, and some were going from one town to another for a day or two. There were games of hide and seek and always other girls to play dolls with and visit.

The Morgan family was camped right next to Pansy's wagon. They were traveling on the same road and had a daughter who was exactly the same age as Pansy. Her name was Ginny. Pansy and Ginny quickly became playmates. It was almost like they were sisters. Pansy had always secretly wanted to have a sister. She thought what fun it would be to have a little sister to watch over and love. The two girls became friends right away.

Because the two families were traveling the same direction, one right behind the other, Ginny asked Papa if Pansy could ride in her wagon for a while. "If it is okay with your parents," Papa said. Ginny's parents agreed and the girls excitedly jumped in the back of Ginny's wagon.

The Doll House

As the wagons rolled along, the two girls played with their dolls. Pansy's doll was homemade out of old scraps of cloth and stuffing. Ginny had fancy store bought dolls that looked real and lifelike. Ginny's papa had built a dollhouse for her that was almost as tall as Ginny. It had a kitchen, living room, bedrooms, and a beautiful porch. It was painted in beautiful pink and white colors, on the outside, just like fancy homes in the big cities. On the inside, Ginny's papa had made little tables and chairs and beds just like a real house. The girls had fun pretending, playing, and imagining they were rich ladies in a fancy home. The dollhouse was beautiful. It did not look like their log cabin ranch house in New Mexico. Pansy imagined that this must be how fancy houses looked back East.

After a long time had passed, the girls grew tired of dolls and decided to get out of the wagon and walk along the road. As much as the girls liked playing with dolls, they also enjoyed the outdoors and adventure.

Along the roadside were lots of little hand-sized rocks and pebbles. Pansy was the first one to say, "Okay, Ginny, I betcha can't hit that tree over there with a rock!" Ginny picked out a smooth stone and threw with all her might at the selected oak tree with leaves turning yellow in the crisp, fall morning air. The stone flew toward its target, but fell short in the grass below. Pansy took the stone in her hand and heaved it toward the unsuspecting tree, hitting it square in the middle.

"I did it!" She proclaimed. The game was on. The rules of the game would be three rocks and three tries. No tree was safe from their newly created activity. This is how it was in those days. Children didn't have many store-bought games so they created fun out of their own imagination. For a while, they threw rocks at trees. When that got too easy, they picked out branches. It wasn't long until they were trying to pick off birds sitting on the branches. The birds were safe. None of them were hit. Ginny was more accurate at throwing, but it was clear, that Pansy had the stronger arm and could throw much farther. After a while, they grew tired of throwing rocks at trees and sticks for Star to fetch.

They ran ahead to Pansy's wagon, which wasn't very far in front. Climbing up into the back of the slow moving wagon, they started telling stories. Pansy told Ginny about her Great-Great Grandmother Nancy, who was stolen by the Indians, and Ginny told Pansy about her Uncle, who was a sharp shooter in *Buffalo Bill's Wild West Show*.

Mama overheard their story telling and asked if she could join them. The girls were happy to say "yes" so Mama sat next to them on the soft pillows, at the back of the wagon, offering each of them an apple. Pansy and Ginny sat eating their apples while Mama talked to them.

"Pansy, I don't think we've ever told you the story about your Aunt Virginia and the time her daughter was very sick and almost died, have we?" asked Mama.

Mama explained to Ginny, "Pansy had a very special aunt by the name of Virginia. She had a daughter by the name of Lucy who became very sick. She was so sick she had to be put in the hospital. The doctors examined her and used their knowledge of medicine to try and make her well.

After many days in the hospital, the doctor came in where Aunt Virginia was waiting and said, 'I'm sorry, Virginia, but your daughter has a blood clot in her lungs and there is nothing we can do. She will only live a few more minutes.'

Aunt Virginia rushed to the hospital room where her daughter, Lucy, was lying. The room was dark and cold. Lucy was unconscious and unable to hear or speak. Aunt Virginia sat down in a chair next to Lucy and touched her on the head and prayed to God. She said, 'Lord

Jesus, you made man, so you know how to heal them. Please heal Lucy right now.' That's all she prayed."

Mama continued, "When Aunt Virginia opened her eyes, she saw a bright yellow light shining at the foot of Lucy's bed just touching her feet. She never spoke a word but just watched as the light slowly began to move over Lucy's entire body.

First, the light shone just on her legs, then over her stomach and, finally, over her chest and head. When Aunt Virginia saw the light move over Lucy's body, she just knew that she was healed. She bowed her head and thanked God for healing her daughter. Virginia got up and went back to the room, where she had been resting, to lie down and get some sleep."

Pansy interrupted Mama and said, "This was sort of like when Jesus was with his disciples in the boat on the Sea of Galilee and there was a storm going on, but Jesus was sleeping in the bottom of the boat. He wasn't worried at all about the storm because he knew God had everything under control."

"That's right, Pansy," said Mama. "Aunt Virginia felt everything would be okay. After about an hour, Virginia woke up and went back to Lucy's room. When she came near the door, she could hear high-pitched chatter and visiting going on inside the room. She opened the door to see Lucy sitting up and talking to the nurse. She was asking why she needed a nurse and why she was being kept in this hospital bed. The doctor arrived about that same time, expecting his patient to be dead, but instead found her alive, well, sitting up, and talking.

'This is impossible!' He said out loud, almost as if he were disappointed. He spoke to Aunt Virginia and said, 'There is no possible way this daughter of yours could be alive. She should be dead!' Aunt Virginia told the doctor she had prayed and God healed her. The doctor just shook his head and kept saying, 'But that's impossible.' Aunt Virginia told him, 'Nothing is impossible with God.'"

"Wow!" said Pansy.

Ginny looked at Mama and asked, "Mrs. Hunt, is that story really true?"

"Yes, Ginny, I've met Virginia and her daughter, Lucy, myself."

"So, she really got better, even after the doctor told everyone she was going to die?" asked Ginny.

"Not only did she get better, but she lived for many years until she was a very old grandmother herself," said Mama.

About that time, the wagon came to a stop. The girls had been having so much fun telling stories they hardly noticed how far they had traveled. Papa was pulling the wagon over underneath some tall oak trees, along the road, for the night. They would be setting up camp with the Morgan's for the evening. The girls could hear their fathers talking and removing harnesses from the horses.

Mama told Pansy that it was time to get ready for dinner and that Ginny's mama would probably want her to help in their wagon.

"Mama," Pansy begged, "Could Ginny eat with us tonight?"

"Of course, she can," said Mama, "because we're all eating together." The girls smiled and shouted approval as Ginny headed over to her wagon to help her mama.

"See you at dinner," hollered Pansy.

"Okay, see you then," responded Ginny.

With so many hands around Mama's stove, dinner was ready in a flash. Pansy noticed that the two mothers were enjoying each other's company as much as she and Ginny. When dinner was over, the mothers told Pansy and Ginny they would wash the dishes, so the girls could go play while there was still some light.

Pansy and Ginny didn't have to be told twice but headed, immediately, to the edge of the woods with Star following close behind.

"We're going to explore," shouted Pansy.

Papa responded, "Not too far, girls, and keep Star right with you.

"Okay, we will!" their voices sang in chorus as they disappeared into the woods.

The woods held all kinds of excitement for the girls. There were things to discover. There were all types of plants, rocks, and curious looking insects. Pansy was not afraid of squirmy things. She was always bringing home some kind of unusual bug for investigation.

Along the way, Pansy had collected butterflies and lightning bugs in jars. She loved to hold the jar full of lightning bugs up at night while she was lying in bed and watch them flash their greenish-yellow tails. She also loved the colors of the butterflies, but after a couple of days, she let them go because it just didn't seem right to keep them pinned up when they wanted to fly. One time on the trip, she had seen a *doe with her fawn* lying in the shade of the willow and oak trees that filled the forest. Pansy loved to wander through the forest, near the camp, when they would stop for the night. Star would always be right there like a trusted guard.

As the girls walked along under the canopy of the tall trees, they talked and laughed, and occasionally found a rock to throw at some unsuspecting branch. As they walked deeper into the woods, they came to a clearing, which opened up to a beautiful lake. You never would have seen the lake from the road, as the thick forest hid it. There it was, though. The most beautiful, blue water Pansy had ever seen.

"Maybe, we could go swimming," said Ginny. Pansy was about to say the same thing when, suddenly from behind them, the girls heard Star sounding his low, rusty growl. The one he made when something unexpected or dangerous was lurking nearby.

"What is it, boy?" asked Pansy.

The girls froze in their tracks. Their backs were against the lake and Star was between the girls and the grove of trees through which they had just walked. Pansy's mind raced back to that mountain lion in the night at the log cabin ranch. A cold shiver went all through her. Ginny was thinking, "Why didn't we stay and do the dishes?"

Star grew silent and his body was hunched over like a spring ready to lunge at any moment. Just ahead in the tall weeds that covered the ground, the girls could see something shaking the grass. Now, they were really frightened. Something was in those tall weeds and it wasn't friendly.

Star began growling in his deepest, most rusty, voice. The girls kept backing up toward the edge of the lake. It could be a mountain lion or a bobcat or maybe some other vicious animal. The girls didn't know if they should run or freeze. At that moment, out from the weeds popped a skunk. An angry skunk! Its black and white tail was high in the air as it turned toward Star.

"Jump in the water," shouted Pansy and, without so much as a second thought, the girls dove into the lake just as Star lunged toward his black and white opponent. One more bark and the angry skunk let go his smelly spray. The next sound the girls heard, as they poked their heads out of the lake, was the whining and whimpering of a now, very stinky dog! Star went to the right and the skunk ran to the left.

The water-drenched girls climbed out of the lake and stood on the shore. They could see the victorious skunk running off into the woods away from them, but the air was filled with the reminder that he had been there. The defeated Star now came back to the girls, but as soon as he got close, the stinky smell of his body chased them away. The girls ran back toward the camp with Star right behind them. As they neared the wagons, they began to shout for Papa and Mama.

Poor Star, even after Papa scrubbed him with strong lye soap in the lake two or three times, he still smelled like the enemy he had challenged. Mr. Morgan helped hold Star still while Papa scrubbed him all over.

"You know, Mr. Hunt," Mr. Morgan said, "This black and white dog looks like a big skunk and now he certainly smells like one."

It would be a week before Star was back to normal. For the next few days, he was kept tied up to the back of the wagon so he couldn't get near anyone. Pansy and Ginny finished the night drying out around the campfire until Ginny had to return to her parents' wagon.

Chapter 10

Skunk Lake and Mama's Surprise

Papa and Mr. Morgan had decided to stay just for a few days right here in this spot. Now that they knew the lake was just beyond the trees, it provided water for the horses and cooking, plus a chance to cool off in the middle of the day. The lake also gave the fathers a chance to do some fishing.

When Papa mentioned fishing, Pansy's eyes lit up. She wanted to go, so it was promised that after chores were finished she and Papa, along with Ginny and Mr. Morgan, would head to the lake to catch fish. Papa always carried a couple cane poles in the wagon. They were set up with string and a hook and ready to go to work at a minute's notice. Pansy could hardly wait but, of course, chores came first in the Hunt house even when on vacation. For Pansy, this meant helping Mama with the breakfast and cleaning up the dishes. After breakfast, it was Pansy's job to feed all of the animals.

The horses were given oats from a large barrel attached to the back of the wagon. Each horse received a couple scoops of oats and then, while Papa led the horses down to the lake to drink, Pansy would feed the chickens and, of course, Star. In about an hour, the chores were done and Pansy scrambled into the wagon to retrieve the cane poles for fishing. The scene at Ginny's wagon was almost the same, except Ginny's Papa had a fancy fishing pole that looked very expensive. Together, the four of them headed to the lake, while the mothers pulled out two chairs and sat to visit while sewing and repairing clothes.

In those days, most people repaired their clothes instead of buying new ones. The mothers found it relaxing to sit and visit while working with their hands. Pansy kept noticing how Mama and Mrs. Morgan were discussing something that seemed very important. They would laugh and then sound very serious. They spoke in sort of hushed voices so they would not be heard. It was, as though, they were sharing some big secret. Whenever Pansy would come close and try to listen, it would always seem like the mothers would start talking about something else. Pansy wondered what was going on, but she never asked. Right now, she was too excited about fishing to think about it any more.

The lake was every bit as beautiful as it had been the evening before, but the faint smell of lingering skunk odor was still present near the place where Pansy and Ginny had jumped into the water. The four avoided that side of the lake and set up at the opposite end where some rocks jutted out over the water making a prime location for sitting with their fishing poles. Papa had brought along a shovel to dig for worms. The worms were used as bait for catching the fish. Pansy loved to watch as Papa's shovel would uncover a chunk of dirt revealing the long, squirmy, snakelike creatures. It was always amazing to Pansy that, no matter where Papa put his shovel in the ground, there would be worms.

"Think about it, Ginny," Pansy said, with a smile. "There are worms just below our feet everywhere we walk." Ginny was less enthusiastic about the worm part of this activity.

"Come on, Ginny!" Pansy begged. "Grab some worms." With that, Pansy stuck her fingers into the rich brown earth and found the first wiggly worm. Papa sat a small can next to them. Into the can went the first worm.

"Your turn, Ginny," Pansy offered. Ginny had a bit of a frown on her face, but reluctantly reached into the dirt, feeling around, until her fingers uncovered the longest, reddish, worm any of them had ever seen. When she grabbed it, the worm wiggled and twisted itself into the shape of a pretzel. Quickly, Ginny dropped the creature into the can. The men laughed at the girls, then they both dug into the dirt clods, finding worms and filling the can with enough worms for the morning's adventure.

Before long, the worms were on the hooks, and the girls were sitting near enough to one another to visit, but not so close that their fishing lines would get tangled. The fathers walked on down the bank, away from the girls, and fished around the lily pads. It wasn't long until Mr. Morgan caught the first fish. Everyone was excited to see him pull the fighting catfish from his watery hole.

"I gotcha," Mr. Morgan boasted with enthusiasm. The fish was placed into a bucket of water with a lid on top to keep it from jumping out. Then everyone went back to their fishing poles. Anticipating the next catch at any moment, the air was filled with excitement. However, after several minutes passed, there was not a single bite. The sun was rising, the air was getting warmer, and the rocks the girls were sitting on were getting harder.

"Where are the fish?" shouted Pansy to Papa.

Papa's voice rang back over the water, "Just be patient."

Pansy had heard that before about being patient. She knew that was not a word she enjoyed. Pansy would rather do almost anything but wait. After an hour, Pansy left her post to go talk to Papa.

"Ginny and I are tired of fishing. We wanna do something else."

"Oh, Pansy," replied Papa. "You have to learn to persevere."

"What does that mean?" asked Pansy.

"Don't give up so quickly. Good things come to those who wait," said Papa.

None of this sounded very good to Pansy, but she reluctantly returned to her post, where she replaced the drowned worm with a new one, thinking maybe a new worm on her hook would interest the fish. Yet, after many more minutes of fishing, no one was catching anything.

Just as Pansy and Ginny were beginning to talk about asking if they could abandon the fishing adventure to go explore, they heard a loud buzzing sound behind them. They turned around to see Mr. Morgan holding a very angry grasshopper between his thumb and finger. He said, "I found this guy in the weeds behind the place where we were standing. Sometimes, if the fish aren't biting on worms, it's because they want something different."

With that, Mr. Morgan lifted Ginny's line out of the water. He removed the worm and stuck the hook through the grasshopper.

"Yuck!" exclaimed Ginny.

"Try that, Ginny," said Mr. Morgan. Ginny tossed the line back into the water and Mr. Morgan said to Pansy, "I'll go find one for you."

Ginny had hardly sat back down on her rock when she felt a tug on the line. "I've got one! I've got one!" Pulling in her line against the powerful tug of the fish was not easy. When the angry fish broke through the water, it sent waves in every direction, splashing with all of its might, trying to escape the hook, which was now firmly snagged in its mouth.

"Pull it up! Pull it in!" shouted Mr. Morgan who had returned when he heard the noise. In a moment, Ginny had landed the biggest fish she had ever seen. Papa and Mr. Morgan told them she had caught a bass.

"It's a beautiful fish," said Papa. Mr. Morgan told Ginny how proud he was of her. With that, both men headed back to get more grasshoppers.

Ginny's Fish

It wasn't long before everyone had caught a fish, but Ginny's fish was the big catch of the day. The girls were so excited, they wanted to go on fishing, but Papa said, "No, we only catch what we can eat today. We have no way of keeping more fish fresh, so it would be wrong to catch them just for the fun of it."

Mr. Morgan agreed. With that, the four of them made the walk from the lake, which they now called "Skunk Lake" to the camp where the mothers were still sitting and visiting.

It wasn't long until the smell of freshly fried fish was coming from Mama's stove top along with the smell of her freshly baked bread. Everyone loved the smell, because it covered up the odor of Star, who was still tied to the back of the wagon. It was fall and the sun would be setting earlier. When dinner was over, they all would be sitting by a crackling fire in the crisp fall air. Pansy loved these nights.

"Wow," said Mama. "Fresh fish from Skunk Lake! That doesn't really sound too appetizing."

"I agree," chimed in Mrs. Morgan. Both women laughed as they served six plates filled with fish, potatoes, bread, and some canned, sweet pickles Mrs. Morgan had stored in her wagon. As they sat around the make shift dinner table, everyone talked and laughed.

Pansy told everyone, "These fish sure did go after those grasshoppers."

Papa spoke up and said, "You know, Pansy, this reminds me of a story about Aunt Virginia and the time the grasshoppers went after her."

"Went after her?" Both girls spoke in unison.

"How is that possible?" Pansy asked.

"Oh, it's possible," agreed Mr. Morgan. "*Grasshoppers* can be very destructive."

"But, they are so little," interrupted Ginny. "What can they possibly do?"

"They are little but, when millions of them show up, they are like an army," Papa said.

"Tell us the story," said the girls.

"I will, right after you do the dishes," said Papa.

"Ohhh!" The girls moaned and the rest of the family laughed. "We will be waiting around the fire."

The girls got the dishes done in record time although, after inspection by Mama, two of the pans had to be returned for further scrubbing. They washed their hands and settled down by the campfire to hear Papa's story. Papa had already explained to the Morgan's about Aunt Virginia and how, on this trip, they had been telling Pansy the many stories about her life. The Morgan's were just about as excited as the girls to hear the story.

Papa began. "This happened many years after Aunt Virginia and her husband, William, had moved to Kansas to become farmers. There was a great drought that swept through that part of the country. All the ponds and streams dried up. Then, all of the crops in the fields dried up and died. This went on for three years until people were desperate. Farmers had *borrowed money from the bank*, expecting to sell their crops to pay it back, but there were no crops to sell. Everyone was starving and had no money. Even Aunt Virginia was in trouble."

"This is a good thing for you to remember, Pansy. Even though Virginia was a good and Godly woman, that didn't guarantee hard times wouldn't come her way," stated Papa.

Pansy spoke up, "You mean like when their house burnt down?"

"That's right. Being a Christian means you trust God to be with you in whatever life brings your way. Just when things seemed like they couldn't get any worse, here came the grasshoppers. There were millions of them, eating everything in sight."

"So they ate her crops?" asked Ginny.

"More than that," said Papa. "The grasshoppers ate anything they could bite. They literally ate the entire back of the shirt her young son, Homer, was wearing while he worked in the fields. They couldn't get away from the grasshoppers.

Some people were having problems because of the drought, so they sold their cows for a little bit of cash, but never paid the bank nor even talked to the banker who had loaned them money. They just used the money for themselves. Virginia bought cows and crops with the money she had borrowed from the bank. The cows were not ready to sell, as they needed to grow more, and the price for selling them at *the market* was almost nothing."

"Now, Pansy, here is where your Aunt Virginia was different from her neighbors," said Papa. "Instead of just selling those cows and keeping the money she owed the bank, she went to the banker and explained what she was planning to do. Her plan was to feed the cows the little bit of *green corn* she had harvested and pray that they would gain weight and grow strong on that green corn, even though all the experts said the cows would probably die eating such young, unripe corn."

Pansy asked Papa, "What's green corn?"

Papa explained, "Green corn is corn that has not ripened and turned yellow. It is too young to pick and it wouldn't taste very good and the experts in that day said it would be harmful to feed to the cattle."

Papa went on. "The banker, who knew Virginia, said, 'Mrs. Rule, you are the first person to come to me in this whole valley with a plan. I know you are a praying woman and I believe your plan will work.'

For many weeks, Virginia's sons fed the green corn to those cows and they continued to grow and become stronger and bigger. Finally, they were large enough to send to market and, by that time, the price had increased so much that Virginia was able to pay the bank what she owed for them plus have enough for her family to live on. This was all because she trusted God and was honest with the banker. While other people ran off in fear and did things which were dishonest, your Aunt Virginia was able to overcome the drought, the low prices, and even the grasshoppers, by trusting God to take care of her and always doing the right and honorable thing."

Pansy spoke up saying, "That reminds me of the story in the Bible where the *three Hebrew children* refused to eat from the king's table but ate only the food God told them to eat. After many days, because they obeyed God, they looked stronger and healthier than all the men who ate the fancy food prepared in the King's palace."

"That's right, Pansy. You have a good memory for Bible stories," said Mrs. Morgan.

"I remember that one, too," said Ginny. "The names of the three Hebrew children were Shadrach, Meshach, and Abednego."

"That's almost right," said Mr. Morgan. "It's Shadrach, Meshach, and "To Bed You Go!!!"

"Ohhhh, not already!" The girls spoke in chorus.

"We have a big day tomorrow," Papa said.

The girls jumped up and went to their wagons. The cool fall air was almost feeling like winter air that night.

Pansy pulled the blankets up tight under her chin as Mama tucked her in for the night. "Mama?" Pansy spoke up. "I've had so much fun with Ginny for the last few days and now, pretty soon, she will be going off in another direction. I'll probably never see Ginny again," complained Pansy.

Mama stood by Pansy's bed and listened quietly to Pansy's heart. "You really enjoyed having a sister for a few days, didn't you, Pansy?"

"Yes," said Pansy in a quiet, sad voice.

"Well, Papa and I have a surprise for you." Pansy looked up wondering. This day had more than enough surprises, but Pansy somehow felt what Mama was about to say was going to be really good.

"Pansy, I'm going to have a baby. You are going to have a little brother or sister," said Mama.

"Really Mama? Are you sure?" asked Pansy. Mama nodded a joyful "yes."

"I hope it's a sister," Pansy stated with great enthusiasm. "When will this happen?"

"Oh, it won't be for a few months," said Mama. "I hope we get back home before it happens but, if not, it will be okay."

"Mama?" Pansy asked as she was being tucked in for the night. "What will we name the baby?"

"Well, Pansy, we haven't thought of a boy's name yet but, if it's a girl, maybe we will call her Bonita. The Spanish people who live all around us in New Mexico use this word, which means pretty or beautiful little one.

"I like it," said Pansy. "We'll call her Bonita."

"Okay, but remember, it may be a boy," said Mama.

"Oh no, Mama, it can't be a boy!" exclaimed Pansy.

"Why not, Pansy?" asked Mama.

"Because I've been praying for a baby sister," said Pansy.

"We'll see, Pansy…we'll see," commented Mama.

Chapter 11

Uncle Will and Heaven

The two families had camped right at the *fork in the road*, which soon would lead them in different directions. The Morgan's would be heading toward their home in Chesterville, Texas, and Pansy's family would push on toward Galveston, which was now only a few more days away. Even though they had only been together for a few short days, the two families felt like they were losing long-time friends as the wagons drifted apart.

Pansy watched out the back of their wagon, while Ginny watched out the back of her wagon. Both girls kept waving goodbye until the curve in the road no longer allowed them to see each other. Pansy sat on the big pillows with a single tear still hanging onto her cheek. She wiped her eyes and nose with one sweep of her hand and looked up at Mama.

"I think Papa wants to see you up front," said Mama.

Most of the time, Papa was the only one sitting on the wagon bench and leading the horses. Occasionally, Mama would relieve him when he grew tired of sitting and wanted to walk for a while. Sometimes, both Papa and Mama would sit and talk, while the wagon rolled along. Pansy couldn't remember ever being asked to come up and sit with Papa as he drove, so she wondered what this was about.

"You better get on up front," urged Mama. Pansy climbed down off the soft pillows, crawled through the opening at the front of the wagon, and onto the seat next to Papa.

"I think it's time you learn to lead the team of horses," proclaimed Papa.

"Really?" Pansy said, with newfound excitement. Papa handed Pansy the reigns and showed her how to hold them.

"Not too tight and not too loose," Papa said. "The horses know where to walk and they'll do most of the work."

Pansy felt big as she held the reigns leading two horses, pulling a loaded wagon, two horses in the back, and one smelly dog.

"This is fun," Pansy told Papa. For a long time, Papa and Pansy sat quietly, while she handled the reigns. Occasionally, Papa would speak to instruct her how to maintain the direction and speed of the horses. Papa was right, though. The horses knew what they were doing and they did most of the work. It was a cool, crisp autumn morning. The sun was shining, but sitting on the bench with Papa made having to say goodbye to Ginny a little easier for Pansy.

As they rode along, Pansy thought of a question she had wanted to ask Papa.

"Papa?" Pansy asked. "You and Mama are always telling stories about Aunt Virginia. You don't talk much about her husband, Uncle William. Why is that?"

"Well, Pansy," Papa began, "What do you want to know about him?"

"What was he like?" Pansy asked.

"Will Rule, as we often called him, was the most fair and honest man I have ever met. I never knew him to lie or cheat. If he borrowed money, he always paid it back plus a little more. He was very caring and helped his neighbors when they had needs. He loved to tell people about Jesus and was faithful to church every Sunday. He always called Sunday the Lord's Day and, on that day, he refused to do any work on the farm except feed and water the livestock, because it was only right to take care of them."

"Do you remember when we told you about the fire when he and Aunt Virginia lost everything they owned?" asked Papa.

"Sure, I do!" said Pansy.

"Some of their friends around the community thought the fire was set by a man who did not like Uncle Will. Many urged him to get the sheriff to go talk to the man but Uncle Will would not accuse him. When people asked him why he would not investigate the fire, Uncle Will would say 'God will take care of us' and he was right. In fact, later on, when that same man was having trouble and needed help, Uncle Will was the first one in line to offer his help. That's the kind of man he was."

Pansy thought for a minute, and then said, "so... so why don't you tell more stories about Uncle Will? Most of the stories you've told me are about Aunt Virginia."

Papa rubbed his chin and looked toward Pansy. There was a sad look in Papa's eyes that she rarely had seen. "Well, Pansy, that's because Uncle Will died and went to be with the Lord while he was still pretty young."

"How did he die?" questioned Pansy.

"Wow..." said Papa. "That's a big story! You remember that Uncle Will and Aunt Virginia had a farm in Kansas?"

"Yes," said Pansy

Papa continued, "By this time, they had six children. You already know about Lucy. Aunt Virginia prayed for her and she got well!"

"Mama told me that story," said Pansy.

"Okay, they also had five other children, Ernest, John, and Wallace and then there was Billy and Homer. Homer was the youngest. He was only nine years old when this happened."

"So, what happened?" asked Pansy anxiously.

"Be patient," said Papa. "I'm telling you." Pansy's grip on the reigns tightened and the horses started to slow down.

"Now, Pansy," Papa said, "If I'm going to tell you this story, you're going to need to relax and just guide the team of horses. Sit back and I'll tell you what happened."

Papa began the story. "One day, Uncle Will came in from working in the field. He told Virginia he didn't feel well and was going upstairs to bed. Now, that was very unusual for Will. He was never sick and, even when he did feel bad, he was the kind of man who would say, 'I'll work, even though I'm sick, and that will help me get better.' He lay in bed for the rest of the day then, later, came down to the kitchen, and told Virginia, 'I'm afraid something bad is going to happen.'

'What?' Virginia asked.

Will said, 'I don't know for sure but something bad and you need to trust God to be with you.'

With that said, he went back to bed for two more days. He began to have a temperature and feel very ill. Aunt Virginia tried to help him. She was like a nurse to many people around the community. Growing up alone on the prairie, there were no doctors close by so she had learned to use *home remedies* that would help people when they were sick."

Papa continued, "Virginia had a very caring heart and would go to other people's houses to help them when they were ill. She did all she knew to do for her husband but he continued to get worse.

Finally, she called for the *doctor*, who rode out to their farmhouse in his buggy pulled by a beautiful, black horse. He came in with his doctor bag and examined Will. He told Virginia he could not find anything wrong with Will but a little fever. He said Will would be better in a couple days.

'No,' said Uncle Will to the doctor and Virginia. 'God has told me that I'm going to die.'

Virginia argued with Will, saying, 'The doctor knows what he's talking about and he said you are not dying!'

The doctor left and Virginia was alone with Will in the room. Will explained to Virginia what God had told him about his dying. He wanted her to know important things like where money was in certain banks and whom she could depend on and trust.

Virginia said to Will, 'you heard the doctor. You're going to be okay.'

'Listen Virginia,' William spoke sharply, 'I know what God has said to me.'

Virginia insisted, 'I know you're going to be okay. God has always taken care of us and He always will.'"

Papa sadly continued, "This upset Aunt Virginia very much, of course. She went downstairs and gathered her children in a circle. They all prayed for their dad. The next day the doctor sent his nurse out to sit with Uncle Will and see how he was doing. While the nurse stayed in the room with Will, Virginia was downstairs sitting at the kitchen table thinking about everything her husband had said to her.

Just then, she heard the nurse calling down to her from the room upstairs. 'Virginia,' she yelled, 'Come quickly.'

Virginia rushed up the stairs and burst into the room. She saw Uncle Will lying on the bed and his face looked very red and hot. The nurse was just laying a wet cloth on his head to cool the temperature. When the cloth touched his head, it was like pouring water onto a hot stove. Steam actually rose from around the wet towel. Virginia rushed to his side and the nurse checked Uncle Will's pulse and heart.

Virginia looked at her husband's face, and then looked at the nurse, 'He's gone, isn't he?' Virginia said to the nurse.

The nurse shook her head and said, 'I am so sorry, Virginia. Yes, he's gone.'"

Papa quietly went on, "There was a strange silence that seemed to fill the room. With that silence, there was also a calmness and peace. It was as though the presence of God had come down and filled every corner of that room with the perfect peace that only comes from knowing God the way Will and Virginia knew Him. There were no outbursts of crying. There were no feelings of shock or pain. It was as though Virginia had a calm confidence that her husband was in God's hands of mercy and there was no reason to worry. Virginia and the nurse just sat there in silence.

A few minutes went by, not very long, when all of a sudden, the silence was broken by the sound of a cough coming from your Uncle Will. Then, another cough and his eyes opened. The first words out of his mouth were, 'Virginia, I was there. I died and went to heaven.'"

Papa continued, "Aunt Virginia was so shocked, she hardly heard his words at first. 'Will!' Virginia said, 'You are alive!' For the next few hours, Will told Virginia and his whole family, who were gathered there, what he had experienced in that short time he was dead.

'Virginia,' he said 'death is nothing. People are always afraid of dying, but I want you to know, it is nothing. There is no reason to fear death.'"

Papa eagerly continued the story, "As his family gathered near to him, he told them what heaven is like and what he had seen. He said, 'There are no words to describe how wonderful it is. There is no need of anything or lack of anything. Everything is perfect. I saw people who I have not seen in years since they passed away. I can't even begin to tell you the beauty of the colors everywhere. The most beautiful scene on earth is nothing compared to what it is like there.'"

Uncle Will tells about Heaven.

"Then, Will said something I'll always remember," said Papa. "He told Virginia, 'time is nothing there. If you live to become an old woman before you die, it will seem like only five minutes have passed, and then you'll be there with me.'"

Papa continued, "The rest of that day and on into the night, Uncle Will called his family, one at a time, to his side, and told them not to worry about him because he was going to heaven and they would all join him later after they had lived their whole lives. He reminded them that God is always faithful, and would take care of them, even if he were not with them.

After he had told everyone how wonderful, beautiful, and perfect heaven is; and, after he told each child how much he loved them and instructed them to take good care of their mother, he then told everyone he was tired and wanted to sleep. He closed his eyes and drifted off into the most calm and peaceful rest. Later on that night, when the nurse checked on him, she saw he was not breathing. Again, she checked his pulse and heart. This time, he had peacefully gone away to heaven to stay."

Pansy sat for a while, thinking about the story she had just been told. Papa could see she was trying to think of a question for him, so he just let her think for a while. Papa took the reigns of the horses and led them on down the road. After a long silence, Pansy broke the quiet, saying, "Papa, why would God bring Uncle Will back to life only to take him away again? That seems…. Well…"

Papa finished her sentence, "Mean?"

"Well, yes," said Pansy, "Why would God do that?"

Papa began. "We can't always know why God allows certain things. The next few years were very difficult times on their farm."

"How come?" asked Pansy.

"Well," said Papa. "There was a horrible *drought* followed by a few years when there was no money, jobs, or food. It was a time we call the *depression*. It was a very bad time in America.

Pansy thought. "So that's even worse." She asked, "Why did God take Uncle Will away from Virginia and all his children right when they needed him the most?"

Papa sighed a little and started again. "Like I said, we don't always know why God allows the things He does, but this is what I do understand, no matter how hard times were, Virginia and every one of Will's children never forgot what he had told them. I think his coming back from the dead gave them strength to trust God and never doubt His love no matter how difficult life seemed to be for them. There were times when they had to trust God for their next meal, but they never went hungry. They always had enough for themselves and a little extra to share with others. During this time, many others were starving and losing everything they owned. What Uncle Will told his family allowed them to see life in a bigger way."

"What do you mean?" queried Pansy.

"From then on, they all knew this world was more than the everyday work and struggle of living. They knew they were headed to a bigger and better place. They were, eventually, going to an eternal place with God. So, when bad times came along, they always knew there was more to life than the tough times they were experiencing now. They knew there was a great reward waiting at the end for those who believed in and trusted God."

"Tell me more about that, Papa," said Pansy!

"Not now, daughter," said Papa. "Maybe we'll save that for when we get to Galveston Island."

"When will that be?" asked Pansy.

"Not long," Papa replied, "not long."

Chapter 12

Galveston Island

After many weeks and almost a thousand miles of bumping along dusty Texas roads, Papa pulled the wagon to a stop. Up ahead was the longest bridge any of them had ever seen. The bridge was made of wood and stretched for two miles connecting Galveston Island to the mainland. The blue gulf water spread out on every side while puffy white clouds painted the blue sky above. There was a light, balmy breeze blowing in their faces, as they poked their heads out of the front of the wagon. Other wagons, buggies, and even some of the new motorcars, were filling the bridge coming and going, to and from the Island.

"Pansy," said Papa in his teaching voice. "You are about to see more people and more activity than you've ever seen in your life. Galveston is one of the busiest shipping ports in the south."

Of course, Papa was right. Back at the log cabin ranch house, they might have a neighbor drop by every few days. They seldom saw strangers. They were about to cross a busy bridge onto an island with non-stop action and activity! Pansy's heart raced at the thought of what awaited them just across that bridge.

Papa whistled to the horses and pulled the wagon out into the traffic on the waiting bridge. The horses' hooves made a loud clompity-clomp-clomp sound as they pounded on the wooden planks. No sooner had they pulled onto the bridge, than a sound coming from behind them began to grow louder. Papa was about to lean around the edge of the wagon to see what was coming, when they all heard the blast of a horn.

BEEP BEEP!!! It startled the horses and it was all Papa could do to keep them walking straight. BEEP BEEP!!! Again, it sounded, as one of the new motorcars swooshed around them.

"Darn new fangled machines!" said Papa, with a look on his face of anger mixed with a little concern.

"Papa!" Pansy spoke up with excitement in her voice. "That's one of the new motorcars we've heard about. Wow! They are fast!"

"Yes," Papa said, "and obnoxious."

Mama laughed, with a knowing twinkle in her eye. "Pansy, has Papa ever told you about the time he drove a motor car?"

"Really, Papa?" exclaimed Pansy.

"Now, Mama," said Papa, "there is no need to talk about that!"

"I think it's a cute story, Papa," said Mama with a lighthearted laugh in her voice. "On one of your father's trips to Silver City, he ran into an old friend who had just bought one of these new machines."

"Really?" said Pansy. "Why didn't you ever tell me? Did you get to ride in it?"

"Oh no, Pansy," said Mama. "More than that, he drove it." Papa looked disapprovingly, as Mama continued, "The man told him how to start it and steer it..."

Papa interrupted, "But, he forgot to tell me how to STOP IT!!!"

"Yes," said Mama, still laughing. "So Papa's friend told him to go down the street and park it in the shed by his house. Papa took off and did just fine until he got to the shed."

"What happened then?" asked Pansy.

"As he came close to the shed, his friend noticed he wasn't slowing down. 'Slow down, George!' yelled his friend. 'Push the brake...Push the brake!!' he hollered. Not knowing what to do, Papa started yelling, 'Whoa! Whoa! Whoa! Like it was a horse.'" Mama was laughing so hard, she hardly could tell the story.

"Then, what happened?" asked Pansy.

"He drove right through the back of the shed still hollering, 'Whoa!'" Now both Pansy and her mama were laughing!

"It's not funny!" demanded Papa. "I had to pay for fixing that shed."

"I know, I know," said Mama in a sweet and understanding way, "but the story is almost worth what we had to pay."

"Maybe for you," said Papa, "not for me!" Despite his angry tone, Pansy could see a hint of a smile around Papa's eyes. She knew he really thought it was funny, too.

They moved steadily across the bridge. Other motorcars passed them, but not with such loud beeping horns like that first one. Even a few fast buggies sped by on their way to do business on the Island. The Hunt family clomped along with beds hanging from the sides of the wagon and chickens clucking underneath. "No one would have to wonder if we were from out of town," thought Pansy. Eventually, they came to the end of the bridge and they were on Galveston Island.

The traffic on the bridge was nothing compared to that on the main street of the city. Pansy's eyes strained to take in everything she was seeing. Huge palm trees lined the main street. Beautiful, exquisite Victorian style houses, like the dollhouse Ginny's papa built for her. Motorcars were everywhere, zipping up and down the wide passageway, through the city. A trolley car, pulled by horses, went up and down the middle of the street loaded with well-dressed passengers. By now, both Mama and Pansy had crawled out onto the seat of the wagon to get a view of everything. The tall buildings, that looked like they reached to the clouds, awed Mama.

Pansy's eyes were drawn to something else. She had spotted a candy store. "Wow!" she thought to herself. "A whole store filled with nothing but sweet candy." Back at the ranch, such things were rare treats. Sometimes, Papa would bring some peppermint sticks or licorice from his trips to Silver City. The sight of that much candy in one place, at one time, astonished Pansy.

"You looking at something, Pansy?" Papa said, as he watched her staring at Miss Polly's Candy Delights.

"Oh, nothing," said Pansy. "Just looking around. There is so much to see."

Papa laughed and said, "I am going to pull over here at *Moore Brothers Feed & Supplies* to pick up some things we're going to need for camping. Why don't you and Mama walk across the street and check out Miss Polly's Candy Delights?"

"Really!" Pansy exclaimed in her most excited voice.

Everyone laughed as they climbed down from the wagon. Papa tied up Star to the wagon wheel and headed into the supply store. Mama and Pansy headed across the street.

Even from outside the candy store, the smell of sweet chocolate mixed with a thousand colors of various kinds of candy delights, filled Pansy's senses until she was almost dizzy with delight. Even Mama was taken back, and a little overwhelmed, at the sweetness of Miss Polly's Candy Store. Miss Polly, the owner, stood behind the counter with a big smile on her face. Pansy hardly heard Miss Polly greet them as she entered the store. "Welcome to Polly's. May I help you ladies?"

Behind the counter was a large glass window. Beyond the window was another large room, where you could easily see dozens of workers busily making every imaginable kind of candy delight. They were mixing large *vats* of chocolate and caramel on one side of the room, and baking colorful rock candy in the far corner. Pansy could see a large table in the center of the room with stacks and stacks of candy canes piled up like a mountain. A worker was loading these into boxes to be sent to other stores in far away cities.

"What do you want, Pansy? Pansy? Pansy?" Mama's words sounded like a far away echo until, finally, Pansy awoke from her dizzy daydream long enough to realize Mama was calling her. "Pansy! What do you want?"

"Sorry, Mama," Pansy replied, "I was just looking at everything. It's all so wonderful." Both Mama and Miss Polly laughed, as they realized how overtaken Pansy was with all the candy.

"I've never seen anything like this," Pansy exclaimed.

In front of Miss Polly, was a glass case with colorful candy sticks. After looking for a while, Pansy selected three colorful candy sticks that were orange, blue, and red with white stripes. She kept two of them in a sack for later, but started on the red and white striped one right away. The sweet taste was heavenly to her. Mama selected a couple chocolate candies and, together, they headed back to the wagon, after thanking Miss Polly.

Meanwhile, across the street, Papa was getting to know Mr. Moore in the feed store. Mr. Moore was a friendly businessman who always smiled and greeted his customers by name. When he saw Papa, he immediately recognized that this man was new to his store.

"Welcome, Sir!" he said with a broad smile on his face. "My name is Mark Moore. I don't believe we have met before."

Papa smiled just as broadly and answered back, "Hunt," he said, "George A. Hunt." As the two shook hands, Mr. Moore could see Papa's wagon and team of horses out in the front of the store. It was obvious to Mr. Moore that this man was traveling and had come from a long distance. The way the wagon was loaded down, Mr. Moore thought Papa might be moving his family to Galveston, so he asked, "Mr. Hunt, it looks like you are loaded up to move. Are you planning to settle here in Galveston?"

"No, no," answered Papa. "We are taking a year-long trip from Lincoln, New Mexico, to Galveston and returning in a few months.

"Lincoln, New Mexico!" exclaimed Mr. Moore. "That's a long, long trip." For several minutes, Mr. Moore and Papa talked about the long journey and some of the adventures getting here. They were laughing loudly, about the skunk story, when Mama and Pansy walked through the door.

"What's so funny?" asked Mama.

Mr. Moore tipped his hat and said, "You must be Mrs. Hunt, Ma'am. It's a pleasure to meet you."

"And you must be Pansy?" he said, as he smiled broadly toward Pansy.

"Your father and I were just talking about the adventure on Skunk Lake and your smelly dog!" Everyone laughed.

Mr. Moore welcomed them all to Galveston and his store. After awhile, they gathered the supplies needed, and Mr. Moore helped Papa load them into the wagon.

"By the way, George," Mr. Moore said. "I know you are planning to camp on the beach, but I see your wife is in a *motherly way*. If you're planning to be here long, I have a real nice house for rent over on 2002 Avenue N ½."

"That's a strange name for a street," answered Papa.

"Maybe so, but it's a beautiful street and only a couple blocks from the beach. Here is the address." Mr. Moore said as he handed Papa a scrap of paper on which he had scribbled down the address. "Go by and look at it if you think you're interested." With that, the two men shook hands, and Papa climbed up onto the wagon bench.

Papa yelled, "Yah!" And with a crack of his whip, the two horses began to pull away from the feed store and down the street leading to the ocean.

Galveston Island Beach

Pansy was still licking the colorful stripes off her candy cane when Papa told everyone to look ahead. There, in front of them, the road ended and the sandy beach stretched out to the left and right forever. Straight ahead, was the Gulf of Mexico. The water was blue as the eyes of a Siamese cat. Out on the water, there were all kinds of boats and ships. The big sailing vessels were making their way into the port to unload goods from all over the world. There were also beautiful sailing ships, quietly slipping through the water, with the ocean breeze filling their sails. It looked like something out of a dream, Pansy thought to herself.

It was so beautiful, she hardly noticed how the beach was full of people getting in and out of the water. On the beach was a little *corral of horses*. People were renting horses, by the hour, to ride along the beach. Up and down the beach ran a road as far as the eye could see. Along the road were all kinds of *shops and merchants*.

Papa turned the wagon to the right and started down the road, which led west along the beach. Papa broke the silence, "Mr. Moore told me to go right and drive on along the beach for about six miles until we come to a campground where other travelers are camping. There will be water there for the horses and other facilities. We can camp there tonight.

For the next few minutes, the Hunt clan just rode along, soaking in the beautiful scene. The sun was bright and the air was warm, but not too hot. The ocean wind, which constantly blew against them, kept everyone comfortable. Pansy commented on the lazy sound of the waves lapping up against the rocks here and there on the beach.

About a mile down the road they came to the largest, most fabulous hotel any of them had ever seen. The sign on the front said *Hotel Galvez*. It reached up several stories above the ground with windows and little balconies facing the Gulf of Mexico in every room. On the side of the hotel was a large *round ballroom* with glass windows all around where people came for fancy parties and special gatherings like weddings and dances.

Pansy was still trying to take in the beauty of the hotel, when Papa spoke up saying, "Pansy, look over there! What do you think of that?" Across the street from the hotel was a sight that was almost too incredible for Pansy's eyes to believe. On the beach, was an enormous *Ferris wheel*. It was filled with people riding round and round, with more folks standing in line waiting their turn. Pansy wondered how she had missed seeing this enormous contraption. Pansy had seen a picture of a Ferris wheel but had never really seen one before with her own eyes. Everyone looked like they were having great fun!

Mama looked at Pansy's eyes and, instantly, knew what she was thinking. "Maybe later, Pansy, maybe later." Mama said with a smile.

It was all so busy, so colorful, so noisy, and so different from home. Pansy had now climbed out of the wagon and was walking along with Star at her side. At that moment though, for some reason, right in the middle of all the excitement and activity, her mind drifted away to the log cabin ranch house. She wondered if everything there was all right. As beautiful as all of this was, Pansy was aware how much she missed the old ranch and how she loved living on the prairie more than anything. Galveston was wildly exotic, but the prairie was home.

Chapter 13

Tucker Island

It took almost an hour to go the six miles along the beach, which brought them to the campground. As Papa guided the horses into the campground, they rode under a huge sign, which read "The Island Campground where Strangers and Travelers are Welcome!" Papa led his team of horses to the camp office where people went to pay the owner for their stay.

While Papa was gone, Pansy began to spy out the neighborhood from her perch on the pillows, looking out the back of the wagon. The camp was filled with tents of every size and shape. There were also a few covered wagons a lot like theirs but none of them had beds hooked on the sides or chickens hanging underneath. Pansy laughed every time she thought of how silly they must look going down the road.

Pansy climbed out of the wagon and whistled to Star. "Let's go, boy," she shouted and Star quickly took his place next to Pansy.

Pansy asked Mama if she could walk over to a little park right in the center of the campground. It was only a short stroll from the camp office, so Mama gave her permission to go to the park. Pansy was hoping to find other children, but the park was completely empty. Later, they would learn that most of the people living at the campground were workers who had jobs in the Galveston shipyards or warehouses along the docks. Many of them were single men without families. This is why Pansy and Star found the park empty.

There were swings and other playground equipment. Pansy saw the tallest slipper slide she had ever seen, but no children were playing in the area. Not a single one. Pansy thought to herself how lonely swings look when there are no children to sit on them. The ocean breeze moved them back and forth lightly, almost as though invisible children were sitting on them and swinging slightly.

Pansy walked up to the swing and was about to sit in it, when a voice behind her called out, "You wanna teeter-totter?" Pansy's head swung around so fast her ponytail nearly slapped her in the face. The voice repeated the invitation again. "You wanna teeter-totter?"

This time she saw a boy about her age climbing down or rather dropping, almost falling down, out of a large oak tree. As he bounded down from his perch on a lower limb, his feet made a little cloud of dust that puffed out over his shoes. Pansy was startled, at first, since she thought she was alone in the park.

"Who are you?" the boy asked, having not yet received an answer to his first question.

"I'm Pansy Hunt," she said to this stranger who appeared from the trees.

"Oh . . . well, I'm Joseph but everybody calls me Little Joe," He said.

"Why do they call you Little Joe?" quizzed Pansy.

"Because my dad's name is Joe. So . . . do you wanna teeter-totter or not?"

Pansy now glanced over past the big slide to a contraption that had been built out of wood. It was a long board that rested on a steel bar. One child could sit on the one end of the board, and another child could sit on the other end of the board, and make each other go up and down. By now, Little Joe was already on his end, so Pansy climbed aboard the other end, and they began to go up and down. As they teeter-tottered, the conversation went something like this.

Joe: "You just getting here?"
Pansy: "Yep."
Joe: "Where you from?"
Pansy: "New Mexico."
Joe: "Where's that?"
Pansy: "Thousand miles away."
Joe: "Is that your wagon over there?"
Pansy: "Yep."
Joe: "It looks funny."
Pansy: "I know."
Joe: Why do you have chickens underneath it?"
Pansy: "To get eggs."
Joe: "Oh . . . (long silence)
Joe: "You like frogs?"
Pansy: "Well . . . I guess, sometimes."
Joe: "Wanna go catch some?"
Pansy: " (A hesitant) Maybe???"
Joe: "Just before the sun sets, there are hundreds of them in the swamp behind the camp."
Pansy: "Hmmmm."
Joe: "My wagon is the last one on the back row next to the well."
Pansy: "Is that right?"
Joe: "Come, after dinner, and I'll show you how to catch them."
Pansy: "Not sure I can . . ."
Joe: "Hey, I gotta go now! Bye."
Pansy: "But . . ."

With that, Little Joe jumped off the teeter-totter while Pansy was in mid air, which sent her crashing to the ground. Pansy's feet caught the dirt just before the crash, softening the blow, as her end of the totter hit the ground. Holding on, she looked up the board to the now empty seat on the other end. In the distance, Little Joe was running toward his wagon. As she crawled off the teeter-totter and headed back to the wagon, she said to Star, "That has to be the strangest boy I've ever met in my life!"

By the time Pansy and Star arrived back at the wagon, Papa had finished his business and was climbing up on the seat, ready to get a campsite for the night. Papa tended to the horses and campfire, while Mama and Pansy fixed dinner. Tonight would be fried chicken and fresh vegetables.

Mama told Pansy to go under the wagon and pick out a chicken and bring it to her. Pansy knew just what to do. She had done this before on the ranch. The selected chicken would become tonight's dinner. "Sorry, girl," she said, as she plucked a cackling hen from out of the cage. Holding the squawking bird, she handed it to Mama.

Pansy didn't like this next part. Mama laid the bird down and, with one swift swoosh of her big knife, it was over. Mama washed off the bird, dipped it in a pot of boiling hot water, then handed it to Pansy for plucking. It was Pansy's job to pluck out every feather until all that was left was a pinkish, naked, headless bird. Surprisingly, this job was not so unpleasant to Pansy.

"Ready!" Pansy called out to Mama. Pansy watched carefully as Mama prepared the meal. From time to time, she would help with the mixing and stirring. Little by little, she was learning to be a wonderful cook like her Mama.

As they set the table with dishes and silverware for the meal, Pansy told Mama about the strange boy she had met in the park and how he liked to go hunting for frogs.

"Frogs!" exclaimed Mama. "Don't bring any of those slimy things around here."

When Papa heard about the frogs, he laughed and told the girls, "Frog legs are good eatin'!"

"They may be good for you George Hunt," cried Mama, "but not good for me!" For some reason, though, Pansy didn't tell Papa or Mama that Little Joe had asked her to go froggin' with him.

After dinner, Papa sat back in his chair and let out a big sigh. "Mama," he said, "that was a wonderful dinner."

Papa looked at Pansy, with a twinkle in his eye, and said, "That's one less chicken returning to the ranch." Then, he gave out a laugh.

Pansy had watched all afternoon for other children to appear from the neighboring wagons and she saw no one, except for an occasional adult, coming and going. Most of the time, it was men who looked like salesmen or dockworkers. Before the sunset, Pansy wandered again into the park. This time, she looked up into the trees with the hope of seeing another child appear. There were none at all. For a while, she sat in one of the swings and swayed back and forth. From her swing, she could look across the road and see the sand dunes and, just beyond the dunes, the sparkling ocean water.

When a large wave would reach the shore, she could hear the crash of water on the beach. Most of the time, though, she just felt the constant, unending ocean breeze. There was something soothing and sleepy about the ocean breeze. Pansy closed her eyes and imagined she was on one of the big sailing ships they had seen as they were traveling along the shore. She rocked her swing from side to side and pretended she was navigating the ocean waves.

"Are you ready to go?" Sounded the familiar voice behind her.

"Huh?" Pansy turned around. This made the second time today this boy has startled me, thought Pansy.

"Go where?" Pansy snapped back.

Little Joe's voice never changed. It was always a monotone matter-of-fact sound, never too excited, and never too much expression. It was sort of a flat, plain voice that answered, "Froggin'! It's time to go froggin'!" Pansy hadn't noticed the long stick in Little Joe's hand. At the end of the stick was a sharp nail, which stuck out of the wood.

"Here," said Little Joe. "You take my pole. I've got another one at my wagon." Almost without thinking, Pansy found the pole in her hand and felt her legs following Little Joe toward his wagon. Maybe it was the boredom of no other children or maybe it was her love for adventure. Maybe it was a little of both, but in a couple minutes they were walking together through the tall marsh weeds that stretched for miles behind the campground.

"We're lookin' for big ones today," said Little Joe.

Pansy was wondering why she had left Star tied up at the wagon. The sun was getting low in the sky and Pansy knew she would be expected back before long. As they pushed ahead, the grass began to get taller and taller, thicker and thicker until it was as tall or taller than either she or Little Joe. Little Joe didn't seem to be bothered by any of this, but just kept on pushing ahead, never saying a single word.

Pansy could see that Little Joe was following a trail of some kind. "Have you been here before?" she asked.

"Of course," was the short, hollow flat reply.

Then, as though some colorful light went on in Little Joe's head, he spoke, for the first time, with excitement! "In just a minute, you are gonna see something beautiful." It was the most expression she had ever heard in his voice.

Part of Pansy wanted to turn around and rush back to the wagon, but another part of her wanted to see what this strange boy thought was so special. On they pushed, just a little more, when all at once they popped out of the tall brush which opened up to the bayside of the Island. It was calm as a lake and blue as the sky.

"See, I told you it was beautiful," Little Joe proudly proclaimed.

Pansy had to admit it was a lovely sight, especially with the sun setting in the background, creating colorful rays of light on the water.

"Let's go!" Little Joe interrupted her thinking.

"Go where?" questioned Pansy. Then, she saw what Little Joe was talking about. There on the shore was a boat, if you could call it a boat. It was small, old, and probably abandoned. It had once been painted white with green trim, but now all the paint was peeling and it looked in terrible shape.

Again the command came from Little Joe, "Let's go! Hop in!" By now, Little Joe had grabbed the stern of the vessel and was ready to launch it to sea.

"That doesn't look safe," said Pansy. "Besides, where are you intending to go?"

"To my island," said Little Joe.

"Your island?" Pansy almost laughed.

"Don't laugh. I've been there a lot of times. We can be there in ten minutes. It's where all the big frogs live." Pansy looked at the boat and looked out at the water.

"We'll be back before the sun sets," Little Joe offered his promise.

Before she thought about it, Pansy was in the boat and the two of them were paddling toward what looked like a sand dune in the middle of the bay. In fact, it was a place where sand had built up into a little island in the middle of the bay with grass and a few little trees. The bay was only about two miles across and the island or "Tucker Island" as Little Joe called it, since his last name was Tucker, was only a mile or so from the shore.

As they paddled, Pansy noticed the water was getting deeper and deeper. "Come on, paddle," said Little Joe to his shipmate.

The Trip to Tucker Island

Pansy began to stroke the water. As the land began to slip away behind them, Pansy had that sort of uneasy feeling you get when you know what you're doing might not be the best idea. Being adventurous, though, she shook off that worry and began to paddle vigorously away from the shore and toward a little hump of sand that stuck up out of the water a long ways ahead of them.

As she paddled, Pansy was taking in all the sights and sounds of the Galveston Bay. Sea gulls were soaring overhead and an occasional fish could be seen jumping out of the water, making splash circles reaching out in all directions. The breeze on this side of the Island was not as strong, but still enough to whistle through her hair. It wasn't long until the shore in front of them was closer than the one they had left. Pansy could see little scrubby trees and green grass here and there growing out of the sand although it was more like weeds than grass. It was easy to see that this was an empty island with no living person on it.

It was precisely at this moment that something horrible began to happen. About fifteen minutes into their trip, the bottom of the little boat began to fill with water. Pansy saw the water first and, with alarm in her voice, told Little Joe. The two of them paddled faster and faster trying to reach the island shore before the boat filled with water. At first the water just covered the floor of the boat, but pretty soon it had risen to their ankles.

"Paddle faster," said Little Joe! The island was only about a hundred yards away but, by now, the boat was filling faster than they could paddle. The weight of the water in the boat made it almost impossible to make progress. The boat was sinking fast. Only a few yards away from the shore, they had to abandon ship. Out of the boat they both jumped, and began to swim to the shore. They made it, just in time, to look back and see the last little point of their wooden watercraft slip under the waves.

"We're stranded on an island," cried Pansy! "Why did I get in that awful boat with you?" They both stood on the shore, soaking wet. Pansy wanted to cry, but instead she instinctively yelled, "Papa!!! Mama!!!"

"They can't hear you," said Little Joe, "we're too far away." Pansy and Little Joe sat down on the sand, looking across the long stretch of sea that now separated them from home. Pansy thought for a moment, then with hope in her voice, said, "Your parents! Do they know you're over here?"

"Uhhh well . . ." Pansy knew by the way Little Joe began that she wasn't going to like this answer. "I live with my dad. He works in the shipyards. My mom died a few years ago when I was little, and I just hang around the campground during the day. One day, I was exploring the area and that's when I found the boat."

"So, have you ever really been here before?" Pansy asked.

"Oh, yes. Look over there." Little Joe pointed toward a place further down the shore and away from the water. "You can see a shelter I made out of old fallen limbs. Looking in the direction where Little Joe was pointing, she saw the most horrible looking shelter she could imagine. It was a *lean to* of sticks with leaves and weeds covering it for shade.

"Sometimes I come over here and just lay in the sand, watching the barges and sailboats go past. Pansy's mind jumped! Barges and sailboats! She stood up, looking in every direction, ready to wave or yell at the first passing vessel.

"Not likely tonight," Little Joe spoke now, in that same monotone sound from earlier. "The barges stop running at *dusk* and it's not likely any pleasure boats will be out after dark."

"You mean we're stuck here," cried Pansy! "My parents will be beside themselves with worry."

For a moment, Pansy's mind flashed back to the story she had been told about her Great-Great Grandmother Nancy who was stolen by the

Indians. She remembered how Nancy's parents had felt such pain and agony. She thought to herself, "I will be causing that same pain and worry to my parents because of what I did." Pansy began to feel hot tears rolling down her cheeks. She didn't want to think of how terrible this would be on Papa and Mama. She sat back down and covered her head with her hands.

Now, in a softer, more caring voice, Little Joe said, "Pansy, don't cry, you'll see, I'll get us out of this mess."

"How?" cried Pansy. Even as she responded to Little Joe, she noticed that the sun had now slipped down below the horizon. "It will be pitch dark soon," Pansy said.

"Don't worry about that, Pansy. I have an oil lantern in the shelter." They both stood up and walked over to the make shift shelter. Inside, under some boards, Little Joe pulled out an old lantern filled with oil and a box of matches.

Across the bay, in the campground, Papa had already begun looking and calling for Pansy. "Pansy has good sense," he said to Mama. "She won't wander very far away."

He said this to Mama but, inside, he was beginning to get concerned. It wasn't like Pansy to not show up on time. If she's not here by dark, then there has to be a very good reason. She may be in trouble. Papa thought all these things and much more. As he went from wagon to wagon asking folks if they had seen her, he quickly learned that most of the wagons were occupied by single men, who had been at work all day and seen nothing.

It wasn't long until a large search party was formed. Some of the men went up and down the beach, hollering for Pansy, while others searched through the weeded area behind the campground. They even got as far as the shoreline on the bay side. No evidence could be found of her having been there. By now, it was pitch dark and every man had a lantern as they searched. The few women in the camp had come over to stay with and comfort Mama.

Then Papa got an idea. He rushed back to the wagon and untied Star. "Go find Pansy, boy! Go find Pansy!" he said.

When Papa released Star, he rushed first to the playground circling the swing set and then scampered toward the wagons near the well. Star kept his nose to the ground and continued to sniff for a couple of minutes around the last wagon, and then he seemed to pick up a trail that headed off into the tall weeds behind the campground.

Papa and a few of the men rushed to follow Star on the search. Some of the men said, "It's no use, we've already searched that area." Through the weeds, Star rushed with Papa and the other men right behind him. Star popped out into the opening where the bay waters were and began to sniff along the shore.

Finally, Star stopped sniffing and just sat down with his head on his paws. Papa's heart sank. All the men with him knew exactly what he feared. What if she got into the water and drowned? Papa said nothing but split the men in two parties to go both directions up and down the shore. As he and the men walked along, they raised their lanterns high to give light a few feet off the shore. No one said anything, but everyone knew what they were dreading to find.

Papa cried out to God. "Oh Lord, please keep Pansy safe. Please return her to us!" At that moment, one of the men who had remained back at the camp came running after the search party. Papa stopped and turned, hoping for good news.

Instead, the man told him one of the other father's, Mr. Tucker, just came home from work. His son is missing, too. He is the same age as your daughter and his wagon is the one next to the well where your dog was sniffing around so much. Wherever they are, they have gone off together.

"What's the boy's name?" asked Papa.

"Little Joe." he said.

"Okay, we are looking for two children now, men. Pansy and Little Joe!" Papa's voice sounded firm as he led the charge. For some reason, knowing she had gone off with another child gave some comfort to Papa. "They can help each other," he thought to himself.

Back on Tucker Island, the night breeze had turned cold. The lantern offered little warmth. Unfortunately, the shelter, which was built in the heat of the day to capture the light winds and keep you shaded and cool, now became a pocket of cold, wet air. Pansy shivered in the breeze. Her body shook from both fear and cold.

"Let me show you how to keep warm. Lie down in the sand," said Little Joe.

"Why?" asked Pansy.

"Trust me," said Little Joe, knowing he hadn't given her much reason to trust. "Just try it," he said. Pansy lay down in the sand away from the shore. Surprisingly, it felt warm from having been baked by the sun all day.

"Okay," Little Joe said, "Now, let me cover you up with sand." Before she could object, Little Joe had covered her feet, then legs and body with a heap of sand using his hands like a shovel. It seemed odd, but it was working. She thought that lying in the sand felt like being covered with one of Mama's down blankets on a winter's night. Pansy piled up some sand under her head like a little pillow.

Lying there, she began to relax. She looked up at the stars, which were so clear. They looked as if you could reach out and pick them out of the sky. If it hadn't been for their awful circumstances, this would have been a beautiful night.

As she lay there, she remembered the many stories she had been told on this trip about trusting God to take care of you. She thought about how God had taken care of her great-great grandmother in much worse circumstances and how, all of her life, Aunt Virginia had trusted God and depended on Him.

Instantly, she sat up from her sand bed and said to Little Joe. "We need to pray!"

"What?" Little Joe replied.

"We need to pray, and right now, that God will help us, send help, or just take care of us somehow," Pansy said insistently.

"Oh…" said Little Joe. "I don't know much about praying."

"That's okay. It's easy. You just tell God what's wrong and ask for His help," she said.

"That sounds easy," answered Little Joe.

"Okay, then let's pray," Pansy urged. Pansy bowed her head and Little Joe followed along.

"Dear God, I know you can see we are in a real mess. I'm sorry, Lord, that we created this problem by not telling anyone where we were going and what we were doing. We were wrong not to ask for permission because we knew our parents would have said 'no.' So, Lord, we've been foolish and we ask your forgiveness. Lord, if you will help us get off this island, we would sure appreciate it. We are tired, hungry, cold, and wet, not to mention scared. We ask you this, in the name of Jesus, Amen."

"Amen," Little Joe repeated.

"So, now what?" Little Joe asked.

"We wait," Pansy said with a smile. "And, we trust God."

"Oh? Hmmm, well okay," was Little Joe's answer.

As they sat quietly staring out into the darkness, Little Joe was the first to say, "Listen… what's that?"

Pansy listened. "I don't hear anything."

"Shushhh!" Little Joe responded…"Listen!"

Now, Pansy could hear a distant whoosh-whoosh-whoosh-whoosh. "It's the sound of a fishing boat coming this way," said Little Joe.

"Really," replied Pansy. "Are you sure?" They both jumped out of their sand blankets and rushed down to the shore, straining to see a small light moving across the water slowly. Whoosh-whoosh-whoosh-whoosh, the sound of the engine was growing louder.

"You said boats don't come through here at night," observed Pansy.

"Maybe I was wrong!" Little Joe ran to grab his lantern and began to swing it wildly in the dark!

Both children were hollering at the top of their lungs. Whoosh-whoosh-whoosh-whoosh. The boat was only a little way off the shore. It was plenty close to see their lantern and two small children in the light of it, but the noise of the engine was so loud, there was no way anyone on the boat could hear their voices. Whoosh-whoosh-whoosh-whoosh!!! It was passing them and moving on down the water with the whoosh-whoosh-whoosh-whoosh beginning to fade.

"No, no," cried the two stranded travelers, "They can't see us. They are leaving us behind."

Then, suddenly, silence! The engines stopped. For a moment, there was no sound. Then, the engine started again with more of a floosh-floosh-floosh-floosh sound. At first, Pansy wasn't certain, but it almost looked like the fishing vessel was moving in reverse.

Little Joe called out, "It's coming back! It's coming back!" Sure enough, in a couple minutes, the boat had backed up toward the shore several hundred feet. The kids could see the name of the ship "Glory" on her sides. Floosh-floosh-floosh-floosh, stop!

A voice called out from the deck, "Are you kids okay?"

"No! Our boat sank and we're stranded here!"

Again, from the deck of the boat, a voice called, "Can you swim out here?" The voice from aboard the ship didn't have to ask twice. Pansy and Little Joe were in the water and swimming toward the ship. Meanwhile, sailors on the deck were throwing lifelines overboard for them to grab. In three minutes, both Pansy and Little Joe were safe on the deck of the fishing vessel named Glory.

The seaman who had called out to them from the deck of the ship told them to stay there and wait for the Captain. Moments later, Captain Eddie stepped out of the bridge and walked down to the two water-soaked strangers. Captain Eddie was an enormous man with a stubbly beard and a white captain's cap that tipped down lower on the left side of his head. The hair over his eyes stuck out wildly in every direction and, when he laughed, he shook everywhere all the way down to his toes. The strangest thing, though, was the odd way he talked. He kind of spoke English, though at times, Pansy wasn't certain. When the Captain walked up to Pansy and Little Joe, he towered over them, and with his booming voice began to speak.

"Aye, you two." He sounded out in a voice as large as his enormous frame. "How'd you get yerselves stranded on that thar sand dune yee this late in de middle of da night?"

"Well, Sir," Little Joe began…

"Speek up ye youngster. Cap'n Eddie don't hear so well with me one good ear."

Then, the Captain let out a laugh. This is when the children first noticed, sure enough, Captain Eddie had only one ear. This explained why his cap sat so slanted on his head. Pansy began to wonder if they might have been safer on the island. This Captain sounded more like a pirate than a ship captain. Meanwhile, they could hear the motors begin to run again with their whoosh-whoosh-whoosh-whoosh sound.

"Oh, Captain Eddie, Sir," Pansy began. "Please, Sir, could you drop us off on the other side, on the island side, so we can get home?" She continued, "We, we, well… our little boat sank and we had to swim to that sand dune. Our families must be sick with fear looking for us."

Captain Eddie

The Captain rubbed his scrubby chin, as though deeply considering the matter. "Ye say yer boat *foundered* in these here waters?"

"No, Sir," Pansy responded, "it sank." The Captain let go another hardy laugh, as did his crew who had gathered all around.

"Which one of ye two is the Captain of yer vessel?" asked the Captain.

"That would be me," said Little Joe in a somewhat more timid voice.

"What be yer name, Captain?"

"I'm Little Joe, Sir."

"Well, Captain Joe, as one captain to another, I'll be obliged to help ye out. Ye be lucky tonight. We ne'er ever sail at night, but we were hed up with enjun truble in de Freeport er we'd be hum in bed by now."

With that, Captain Eddie turned to the helmsman and yelled out, "Bring er about, Mate. "We be going to the Far Shore!!!" No sooner had the Captain hollered out the order, than the fishing ship began to turn around and head toward the Island shore.

Suddenly, Pansy's heart was filled with the understanding that this was no accidental encounter. She realized that God had heard her prayer as sure as He had heard the prayers of her Great-Great Grandmother Nancy, Aunt Virginia, or her own Papa and Mama. She understood in that moment what her parents had been teaching her through those stories for the last thousand miles. "Trust God with all your heart and He will always be with you."

The engine trouble the Captain experienced in Freeport was the way God delayed this kindly Captain so he could be, at the right place and just the right time, to rescue two foolish children who had gotten themselves in a mess.

Pansy closed her eyes and said, "Thank you, Lord!"

In just a few minutes, they were moving close to the shoreline of the Island. Pansy and Little Joe had been given blankets in which to wrap themselves. Even with the blankets, they were shivering to the bone. Standing on the deck of the boat, they looked ahead to the beach area and could see dozens of lanterns moving and waving up and down along the shore. Pansy realized this was probably a search party looking for the two of them.

As the boat came near to the land, the engine stopped and the Captain picked up a large megaphone. From the bridge of his ship, he hollered to the men moving about on the shore. "Do ye men be lookin' for two youngsters?"

A dozen men yelled back, "Yes, Sir!"

"They be here on my deck!" said the Captain.

Quickly, two of the men in the search party jumped in a waiting rowboat, while others ran to find Papa Hunt and Mr. Tucker.

The shipmates lowered Pansy and Little Joe down the side of the ship and into the waiting boat. One of the men in the boat asked the two of them if they were okay, while the other spoke to Captain Eddie, asking him to wait for the fathers to come.

"I know they'll want to thank you!"

"Tell dem faters that the youngsters be safe and sound and that be tanks enough. We be shovin' off for home now." With that, the Captain signaled to his Mate at the helm and the engines began to whoosh-whoosh-whoosh-whoosh again! Off the Captain went into the darkness of the night.

Pansy and Little Joe were now standing on the shore and hollering back to Captain Eddie their thanks. The fishing boat sounded its horn three long times and the men on her decks waved back.

No sooner had Captain Eddie slipped into the darkness than the two anxious fathers came popping out of the brush.

"Pansy!" Papa cried out and threw his arms around her.

Mr. Tucker, who was just steps behind Papa, knelt down in the sand and put his hand on Little Joe's shoulder. "Don't ever do this again, Son. Where on earth have you been? All these men have been searching everywhere for the two of you."

Word spread quickly around the campground that the children had been found and they were wet, but okay. Mama just sat down and wept with relief. Of course, the whole story had to be told over and over until everyone had learned what happened. After hugs and kisses, warm clothes were put on and warm food was put into the two children. Talk about discipline would be delayed until tomorrow. Tonight, everyone was rejoicing that this story had a happy ending.

The family would stay on the Island for several weeks before heading home. During that time, Papa would make many attempts to learn whom and where this Captain Eddie was, as he wanted to thank him for rescuing the children. He went to the docks and asked around. He talked with the other fishermen who had worked these waters for years. No one had ever heard of Captain Eddie or of a fishing boat named "Glory."

Chapter 14

1618 West 22nd Terrace

It was decided that the appropriate punishment for wandering off without checking with Papa and Mama would be…well…put on hold for now. This was not the usual way Papa or, for that matter, Mama handled correction around the house. Papa could be stern and demanding. He wasn't afraid to insist on obedience and, if necessary, apply understanding with a switch.

This time, however, both he and Mama were very thoughtful about what had happened. "This has been a very long trip," said Mama. "Even though Pansy is use to playing alone she probably misses her school friends."

"You remember," Mama went on, "how much she enjoyed the company of the Morgan's girl, Ginny? I think she wanted to be with other children so much, it led her to make a bad decision."

Papa had to think about Mama's words for a while. Though he was stern, he was also a thoughtful and forgiving father. He understood that the fear of that night on the island was probably punishment enough. After Papa and Mama talked it over, it was decided there would be no punishment unless something like this occurred again. They turned the lantern out and went to sleep.

On the other side of the wagon, Pansy had already fallen asleep almost as soon as her head hit the pillow. Star was curled up below her bed. Star understood that something bad had happened and he wanted to stand guard all night to protect Pansy.

Across the campground, in the Tucker wagon, Little Joe's dad sat quietly in a chair. He had worried about leaving his son alone all day while he worked at the docks. As he sat there thinking, it bothered him that his son was not in school like other children. He was considering leaving the docks and taking his son back to Missouri, where they had come from, so he could have a more normal life. While he thought on these things, Little Joe had fallen asleep on some soft pillows in the back of their wagon.

The campground was quiet except for the sound of the ocean breeze waving the canvas on the tents and wagons. The moon was high in the sky and the stars were like diamonds scattered across a black canvas. Peace had returned and it was welcomed.

Morning came early for Papa. He was up long before anyone else. He saddled Thunder and rode out of the campground before the sun came up. Not even the clomp, clomp of Thunder's large hooves could awaken Pansy as she slept soundly in her bed.

Mama rose early, too, and began to poke at the fire until she had a small blaze churning under the stove. The smell of bacon and hot biscuits cooking began to wake up Pansy. Crawling out of her bed, she slipped over the side rail and fell down with a plunk, onto the ground below right next to Star. Star lifted his head, as if to acknowledge Pansy for a moment, then went back to sleep.

"Are you hungry?" came Mama's cheery good morning voice into Pansy's ears.

"Yes! I am very hungry!" responded Pansy. The morning began with Mama and Pansy, sitting across from each other, enjoying a big breakfast.

"Were you scared?" asked Mama, "stranded out there on that island?"

Pansy thought, and then answered, saying, "You know, Mama, at first I was angry with myself for getting into that situation. Later, I was scared, but by the time I started to get really scared, I began to think about all those stories you and Papa have been telling me on this trip. I thought about Great-Great Grandma Nancy being captured by the Indians and about all the times God was with Aunt Virginia. I thought to myself, if God could help them in those huge problems, I know He can get me off this little island and safely home."

Mama looked at Pansy with great pleasure and said, "Pansy, that was the Spirit of God, or sometimes we call Him the Holy Spirit, speaking to you and reminding you that He will always be there for you."

Pansy beamed and spoke up. "That's why I stopped right there, and told Little Joe we have to pray. You know, Mama, it wasn't five minutes after we prayed, and that fishing boat showed up."

"You've taken a big step, Pansy," said Mama, "into a new world of spiritual understanding and trusting God for yourself. You see, that's why we have been telling you all of these stories. Not just to entertain you but, more importantly, so you will learn that what God did for your Great-Great Grandmother Nancy or Aunt Virginia, He will also do for you.

Pansy glanced up at Mama with a curious look on her face. "What?" asked Mama, knowingly.

"Well," Pansy began, "there is just one thing about all of this I don't understand."

"What is that?" Mama questioned,

Pansy began by saying "I can understand why God helped Great-Great Grandma Nancy and Aunt Virginia. They were wonderful people and didn't do anything wrong but . . ." Pansy paused, as she thought for a moment, then went on. "It's hard to say, but why did God help Little Joe and me when we were wandering off and doing something we knew we shouldn't be doing?"

"That's a great question, Pansy," replied Mama, with a wise look in her eyes. "Why do you think God would help you, even when the problem is of your own doing?"

Pansy thought for a moment, looked up, and said, "The only reason I can think of is that He loves us in spite of our mistakes."

"That's right, Pansy. The Bible is filled with the stories of people who went down the wrong road, made mistakes, disobeyed God, and more. Over and over, again and again, we see how God forgave and rescued them because of His great love for mankind."

Mama went on. "Pansy, remember all those stories about men like Abraham, Moses, Jacob, David, the Prodigal Son, Jonah, and the Apostle Peter? All of these men had horrible failures in their lives but, in every single case, God forgave them and rescued them. He rescued Abraham from Pharaoh and Jonah from the great fish. He forgave Moses for his anger, David for his sinfulness, and even Peter for denying him."

"You see, Pansy, all these people in the Bible are there for examples. They are true stories of real people going through real life situations, just like Aunt Virginia and Nancy Ross. They are not made up stories, they are true stories about how people made mistakes, but God brought forgiveness, blessing, and restoration. I am so proud of you, Pansy."

"You are?" Pansy responded with surprise in her voice.

"Yes, I am proud to see how your spirit is growing and learning about the truths of God. They will stay with you all your life, Pansy. God has promised to never leave you and to never forsake you."

Pansy thought, then spoke "In just the same way He did with my Aunt Virginia?"

"Yes, Pansy! Just like that. God wants to do, in your life, the same things He has done for others. Aunt Virginia had six children, and I can tell you that every one of them have their own stories of God's help and provision, just like their papa and mama."

"Can you tell me one of those stories?" Pansy asked.

"Well, okay. While we wait for Papa to return from town, I'll tell you the story of Aunt Virginia's son, Homer, and the miracle house."

"Another house story?" Pansy spoke up.

"Well..." said Mama, "God is interested in providing for our needs and a house is a pretty important need."

"That's true," Pansy spoke up. "I enjoy living in this covered wagon but, lately, I've been missing our log cabin ranch house."

"I am sure you have, Pansy, I am sure you have." Mama responded with a smile.

Mama settled back into her chair and began to tell the story of Homer Rule or H.T., as some called him, and the miracle house. "Homer was Virginia's youngest son. When Homer became a grown man, God called him to the ministry. That means he felt God telling him to leave his regular job, which was painting cars, and to devote his whole life to preaching the Gospel."

"About the same time that God was speaking to Homer's heart about all of this, a man from a big factory offered to put him in charge of painting all the vehicles that his company built," Mama stopped to take a sip of her tea then continued. "It was an important job and it would pay a lot of money – more money than Homer had ever received.

Now, Homer had a tough decision to make. He could forget going into the ministry and take this job, which would allow him to be able to provide for his family a much better house and a new car plus many other extras things that people often want.

He told the man from the factory that he would have to think about it, pray about it, and talk to his wife. But the truth was, he didn't have to do any of those things. He knew, deep in his heart, that God had called him away from his old job of painting vehicles to serve Him as a pastor. The next day, Homer called the man from the factory and thanked him for the opportunity, but turned him down, saying he was going into the ministry.

Instead of respecting Homer's decision and choice, the man from the factory got angry with him and began to shout at him over the phone. He told Homer that he was a stupid man for turning down such a good job. He said he hoped Homer would fail in the ministry and he better never come crawling back to ask for a job! When Homer hung up the phone, he knew he had made the right decision. Any man who would react that way would not be a good boss."

"So, a few years went by and Homer had been pastor of several churches. Some churches were very small and didn't provide much money for his family. To put food on the table, Homer often had to do odd jobs around the town. Even then, there were times when there was not enough money to pay the bills and provide for his children," said Mama.

Mama continued the story, "All Homer ever wanted was to do God's work and provide a good home for his family. One day Homer and his wife, Doris, were invited to a special party being given for a family member who had just gotten married. As a wedding present, the bride and groom had been given a brand new home by their parents. The home was in a beautiful, new neighborhood. There were new and partially built houses all up and down the street where the party was being held. Homer and his wife, Doris, went to the party. Homer was happy for the bride and groom but, inside, he was crying.

He had spent his whole life trying to make enough money to buy a house. No bank would lend him the money because he was too poor. His dream of owning a home seemed far away and impossible. While the party was going on, Homer slipped away and took a walk to be by himself for a while. He wandered along the street looking at all the new houses being built, and asked God why he couldn't own one of these homes.

After walking about a block, he came to a place where a house was about to be built. All that was there was the foundation, which is the concrete part on which the house is built. Homer walked over and sat down on the concrete foundation and began to cry out to God. 'Lord, you know what is best, but I'm begging you to please hear my prayer. I've done what you asked me to do. I have given my life to you as a Pastor. I am serving your people in church and trying to obey and hear your voice. I have a family and we need a good home. The houses we've been living in are old and drafty. They are hot in the summer and cold in the winter plus expensive. I want my own home, Lord. I ask you to hear my prayer. Amen.'"

Pansy spoke up, "So, did God give Homer a house?"

"Not so fast," replied Mama. "Now, we're getting to the good part. No… God didn't answer Homer's prayer right away like he did for you and Little Joe on the island. In fact, it was two years before something amazing happened."

Mama continued the story, "Homer ministered at a small church called Faith Church. Like all the other churches he pastored, it was small, so he had to do other work on the side to put food on the table.

Homer worked for a man, who built houses, by the name of Big Bud. Big Bud was a big, tough man who hired a lot of workers to build houses. Many of the men didn't like Bud because he was so gruff and demanding. However, Bud really liked Homer because he was such an honest and hard worker. Big Bud had heard Homer wanted to buy a house someday.

One day, he called Homer into his office. Big Bud called everyone by their last name. When Homer walked into Bud's office, he yelled, 'RULE!!! Get in here!' Homer thought he must be in some terrible trouble.

'I hear you want to buy a house,' Bud said.

Homer shifted his feet a little, then looked Bud in the eye, and said, 'I sure do!' Bud handed Homer a slip of paper with an address written on it. It read, *1618 West 22nd Terrace.*

Now listen, Homer, 'I built this house two years ago and the people who bought it stopped making their payments . . . then, left town. You go by and look at it. If you want it, you can just start making the payments the other people quit making, and it's yours.'

At the end of the day, Homer could hardly wait to get in his old car and drive over to see the house. His head was spinning, as he found the street, and began to drive down it, looking for the address. He recognized that it was the same street where he had gone to that party two years earlier. He watched the addresses on the houses until he came to 1618. As he pulled into the driveway, he could hardly believe his eyes. It was that same house! It was the foundation, where he had sat two years earlier and cried out to God for a home.

Tears ran down his cheeks, as he realized that God had heard every word he had prayed. When the time was right, God provided the miracle house, for which he had been praying. Homer looked up to heaven and cried out, 'Thank you Lord! Thank you Lord! You really do hear us when we pray. You really do care about our needs. Thank you Lord!' Homer moved into that house with his wife and four children. He built a great church and lived in that house and that community for many years. God provided a home for him."

"So, you see, Pansy," Mama said, "you are learning the same things your Aunt Virginia, her son, Homer, and so many others have learned. God promises to walk with us through life and he promises to never leave nor forsake us. We might not get everything we want in life but God has promised to provide for our needs."

Chapter 15

The Big House

Mama and Pansy were just cleaning up from breakfast when they heard the familiar clippity clop of Thunder coming up the road. "Papa's coming!" announced Pansy.

For a moment, her mind swept back to the log cabin ranch house again and the many times she had heard that familiar sound coming up the path to the house. Pansy had been thinking more and more about the old ranch house and missing it lately. They had been gone now for many months. Mama was expecting the baby and everyone was thinking it would sure be nice to be home before the baby was born.

Of course, as usual, Papa always was working on another plan. Papa rode to the wagon and tied up Thunder while Star ran in circles around his feet, begging for a pat on the head. Papa reached down and ruffled the hair on top of Star's head.

He then looked at Mama and Pansy and said, "Are you women ready for a surprise?"

Pansy replied with an excited "YES!"

But, Mama had that "what now" look in her eyes. "I've seen some of your surprises, George Hunt. What are you planning now? Another vacation?"

Papa smiled at Mama and said, "Well, yes, in a way. I've just come from talking to Mr. Moore at Moore Brothers Feed and Supplies. When we were there the other day, he told me about a house he had for rent. He noticed we were expecting a baby and thought you might need to get out of that wagon for a while and into a real house. I thought that was a good idea, so I went to look at it."

Mama looked at Papa and said, "George, what will this cost us?"

"Nothing, Mama! I've agreed to help Mark at the store from time to time and he will let us live in the house in exchange. It's fully furnished with everything from a stove to beds. It's a five-minute walk to the beach from the front door and, when you look out the upstairs window, you can see and hear the ocean. What do you think?"

The thought of sleeping with a roof over their heads, instead of the stars every night, sounded wonderful to Mama and Pansy.

"Can we see it?" asked Mama.

"Of course," said Papa.

As the wagon pulled up in front of *2002 Avenue N ½*, Pansy could not believe her eyes. "It looks like Ginny's doll house!" Pansy exclaimed.

Sure enough, this was a tall Victorian style home that looked just like the fancy doll house her friend, Ginny, owned. Pansy always wondered what it would be like to live in a fancy house like this. It sat on the corner of 18th Street and Avenue N ½, which was a silly sounding name for a street, but that didn't matter to Mama or Pansy. Having a real roof over their heads, for a while, would be welcomed.

Papa said he still wanted to camp on the beach from time to time, so the plan was made that the family would spend most of the time living in the Big House, as they called it, but two days a week, they would take the wagon down to the beach to camp and fish overnight. Sundays were the Lord's Day. That day was reserved for going to a little church near the house and relaxing at home the rest of the day.

The Big House

The first thing Pansy did was look up and down the street for other children her age. She didn't see anyone, but then realized it was a school day, and they were probably in their classes. It didn't take long to move their few belongings into the Big House. Pansy picked out a bedroom upstairs which had a window that looked out over the rooftops of the other houses. You could see the blue gulf waters and, just like Papa said, you could almost hear the sound of the waves splashing against the shore and the wind blowing through the window. The room already had a soft bed, which Pansy looked forward to curling up in later that night, and a dresser drawer with a mirror, where she could place her clothes and comb her hair.

After unloading the necessary items from the wagon, Papa moved the wagon and team of horses to a nearby barn that belonged to Mr. Moore. He had told Papa he could board his horses in the barn and leave the wagon outside where it would be safe. In a flash, the Hunt family went from traveling vagabonds to local residents of Galveston Island, Texas.

By three o'clock in the afternoon, the house was settled and Pansy was swinging in a big front porch swing as the neighborhood children began returning from school. She watched them streaming down the street and entering every house along the way. Pansy was amazed, and thought to herself, "There are more children on this block than attend my whole school back home."

She saw a girl about her age, walking up the street holding her little sister's hand, with what appeared to be another sister and brother following right behind. When they got in front of Pansy's house, the girl stopped, looked at Pansy, and said, "Who are you?"

"I am Pansy," she said. "We just moved in. The girl started up the walk toward Pansy, still holding her little sister's hand. The other two children walked on and went into the house next door. Pansy stood up from the swing and met the dark haired girl at the top of the porch steps.

"I am Annie and this is my little sister, Alissa, but everyone calls her Lizzie." Pointing to the other two children, she said, "That's Mark and Rosalan. We live next door."

"Where are you from?" Annie asked.

"We're from New Mexico. We're just here for a while," replied Pansy.

"I know," Annie responded. "The people in this house are always here for just a little while."

"How did you know that?" asked Pansy.

"This is Mr. Moore's rental house. He always rents it to people passing through Galveston in exchange for help at his store." Annie said.

"Really?" Pansy was a little surprised that she would know this much information.

"So . . . how long are you here for?" asked Annie.

Pansy told her, "Probably just a few weeks, then we will be heading back to New Mexico before Mama has a baby."

Annie asked, "What grade are you in?"

For Pansy, this was sometimes a hard question to answer. She attended a one-room schoolhouse where there were no more than ten or fifteen children of all ages. At times, Pansy had to help the younger children with their lessons.

Annie didn't wait for Pansy's answer, but told her, "I am in the fifth grade."

"So am I," replied Pansy figuring that was about right.

The two girls talked on and on, with Pansy asking questions about Galveston, and Annie asking questions about the far away land of New Mexico. Annie lived on the ocean and Pansy lived in the mountains. Coming from such different places, each one found the other's life interesting. In a few minutes, the two struck up a little friendship and, before Annie left, she invited Pansy to come over and play the next day, since it was Saturday.

The move into the Big House on N ½ Avenue proved to be a wonderful blessing. Mama loved feeling a little more settled, for a while, which prepared her for the two big things which were coming soon, the trip home and the baby. Papa enjoyed working with Mr. Moore at the hardware store. Mr. Moore was always trying to convince Papa to make the move to Galveston permanent, but Papa loved the wide, open land in New Mexico.

He often told Mr. Moore, "You just can't understand unless you are there. It's a beautiful nothingness that stretches for hundreds of miles. Besides, Papa had thousands of sheep and was loved and respected by his neighbors. Papa's roots were in Lincoln and he never intended to leave the ranch. For the Hunt family, New Mexico was home sweet home.

For Pansy, life on N ½ Avenue was unlike anything she had ever experienced. For the next few weeks, she came to know Annie and her sisters, Rosalan and Lizzie, and brother, Mark. Just across the street was an all-girls house. Pansy became friends with all of them; Emily, Hailey, Madison, and Beth. Two doors down, she often played with the Drake twins, Hadley and Jackson. All these children were her age or just a little younger.

In New Mexico, the nearest neighbor, with children, was more than two miles from the ranch. Here in Galveston, you could hear the sounds of playing children in back yards up and down the block. Pansy quickly became part of the neighborhood.

Over the next few weeks, from time to time, Papa would pull out the wagon and hitch up the horses. The family would disappear to the beach for a couple days to fish and catch crab and shrimp. Those days were wonderful. Camping right on the beach, falling asleep to the gentle splashing of the waves against the rocks, and eating all the fish and crab you could possibly want, then coming back to the Big House. It was all quite wonderful.

They even went to the Ferris wheel and Pansy was allowed to ride it two times. Papa refused to get on "that crazy thing" as he called it but, after watching the fun, Mama climbed on with Pansy and they both enjoyed the view from high in the air. Papa probably would have stayed on the beach all the time but he knew how helpful the Big House was to everyone else. Sometimes, when they would go to the beach, Pansy was allowed to bring along one of the other girls in the neighborhood. The next few weeks were the best of the entire trip for Pansy and her parents. Now, a very special day was approaching for Pansy.

Chapter 16

Birthday on the Beach

Today was a very special day. It was Pansy's tenth birthday. After getting permission from neighborhood parents, the children, with whom Pansy had become friends, piled into the wagon, and they all headed to the beach for Pansy's birthday party. While the children played games on the beach and in the shallow waters, Papa and a couple of the fathers went fishing farther down the shore.

Mama and Mrs. Drake watched carefully over this high-energy gang of children, while they prepared the table and began to build a fire for frying fresh fish. The big event of the day was when everyone broke up into teams and built sand castles. It became a contest to see which team could build the biggest, highest, and most fancy castle. Pansy teamed up with Emily; Rosalan and Bethany worked together; Alissa and Hailey became a team; and Annie built a castle with Hadley and Madison. They all were careful and meticulous; making sure everything about their castles was perfectly formed, neat, and balanced.

The two boys, Mark and Jackson, were a team. They built the tallest castle, but it looked more like a sand mountain than a sand castle. By the time the sand castle building was over, the dads' returned with a fresh catch of fish. To Pansy, nothing tasted better than freshly caught fish right out of the ocean, into the pan, and then onto her plate. Soon, the smell of fish frying filled the air. Mama always knew just the right spices to add that would make everything delicious.

The dads' judged the sand castles, and then gathered everyone around the table to sit down and eat. Once seated, Papa removed his hat, as did the other men, and offered thanks to God for the food, a safe journey, and newly found friends. Everyone joined in saying "Amen" and the meal began.

After dinner, Mama brought out the finest, largest chocolate cake she had ever made. They had to brush a little sand out of the frosting but, all in all, it was the best birthday Pansy could ever remember. After the dinner was over and dishes were cleaned, everyone gathered around the campfire for roasting marshmallows and telling stories.

Tonight, Papa told stories of his younger days on the ranch in New Mexico. Papa had lived on the ranch way back in the 1880s. This was a wild time in New Mexico. Not even Pansy knew that Papa had been a deputy sheriff for Lincoln County in those days. Papa told stories about the Apache Indian brave, Geronimo, and Billy the Kid, a famous outlaw.

Every child around the fire had heard of *Billy the Kid* because many stories had been written about him and could be purchased in *five-cent novels*. Most people had come to know the "Kid" as a notorious outlaw who had killed lots of men, most of them bad men who were trying to kill him.

Papa told them he could tell the real story of Billy, because his neighbor and good friend just down the road, *Frank Coe*, had shared the tale with him. Papa explained to everyone that Billy the Kid, whose real name was William Bonnie McCarty, worked for Mr. Coe. Well, this got the attention of all the kids, especially the boys.

Mark and Jackson, both asked, "Mr. Hunt, did you ever meet Billy the Kid?"

Papa answered, "Sure I did. He was just another hired hand who worked on the Coe ranch. All of us ranchers hired young men like Billy. Some of them might have had some problems in the past. We never asked anything about that, as long as they did their job, and followed the rules. McCarty was a good worker, as I recall. When all the trouble started, I left for a few years, so I wasn't there when he got into trouble with the law."

"What trouble, Mr. Hunt?" Mark asked.

Papa answered, "Well, Mark, in those days there were some big ranchers. Mr. Coe was one of them, but there were others, and they were quarreling over who was going to be in charge of the territory around Lincoln. Some people sided with Mr. Coe and his men, while others took up with some other folks. Some were cattle ranchers, but some were sheep ranchers, like me. I could see a war brewing between these two groups, so I sold a lot of my sheep and got out while the getting was good. There were good people on both sides and I didn't want to get in the middle of the war."

"You see, kids, when a war occurs, lots of innocent people get hurt. Sure enough, that's what happened. It turned into an all out war."

Jackson spoke up, "I know, Mr. Hunt, I've read about it! They called it the Lincoln County War."

"That's right, Jackson," said Papa.

"I can tell you boys have done your homework on Billy the Kid. Remember, though, his name was really just William, William Bonnie McCarty. So, let me tell you about Billy. He had it rough growing up. He never knew his father and his mother, whose name was Catherine, died when he was just a teenager. For a while, he had a stepfather, but he was gone most of the time and never paid much attention to Billy or his brother. It wasn't long until Billy began to get in trouble with the law here and there around the countryside.

At first, it was nothing big, but one thing led to another and, before long, Billy was a wanted man running from the law. There are lots of stories about Billy the Kid in his younger days. Most of them are probably not true. What I can tell you is that Billy rode onto the Coe Ranch, looking for work, and my friend, Mr. Coe, hired him. I remember seeing him a couple times but, to me, he was just another one of the ranch hands, that's all.

Then, when the trouble began to stir up in Lincoln, the two sides began to fight and shoot at one another. Mr. Coe was shot and killed in one of the gunfights, which only led to more shooting and killing. Billy got involved, like so many others, only Billy found the man who shot his boss and shot him dead. Billy wasn't from those parts and because he already had a bad reputation with the law, the Sheriff and the Governor made an example of him. He was tried and sentenced to hanging, but broke out of jail, and again was running from the law. Eventually, they caught him. He was shot and killed."

Papa continued, "The thing is, kids, Billy didn't have to end up dead at the age of twenty-two years old. He was a talented young man. They say he was very smart and skillful with his hands. He might have been a captain in the army or worked in law enforcement, using his unusual skills with a gun to catch criminals, instead of being one. They say he was a friendly and interesting person to be around, and a great storyteller. He might have been a salesman or a merchant or maybe a banker.

The trouble with Billy was he didn't have anyone to love him and give him direction in life, like all of you do. He didn't have a church to attend or even a school most of the time. He wasn't taught about God and how to serve Him or how to respect authority. Yes, kids, Billy could have been a lot of good things. Instead, he spent most of his life hungry, miserable, and running from the law. In the end, he was just an unfortunate, unhappy kid who died in a gun battle.

Oh, he's famous, I suppose, just because a lot of writers have made up stories about him to sell to the public, but you know what kids? I betcha, if we could bring Billy the Kid back right now and sit him down at this campfire, he would tell everyone of you to never, never follow in his footsteps. I imagine he would talk about all the good things he could have done and all the people he could have helped instead of hurting them."

Papa's story had captured the attention of every child in the circle around the campfire. Papa was right. The newspapers made Billy the Kid out to be some kind of *folk hero* when, in fact, he was just an unfortunate, young person who came to a miserable and tragic end.

After the story had been told, all the children were sitting around the campfire a little thoughtful and Mama was thinking this is a little too serious for a birthday party. She looked at Papa and said, "Why don't you tell the children about the most famous bear in the world!"

Papa smiled and turned to the kids saying, "Who do you think is the most famous bear in the world?"

The children looked at one another. Some of the kids asked each other, "Who is the most famous bear?" but it was Emily who raised her hand and said, "Mr. Hunt, I know, I know!"

"Tell us, Emily," said Papa.

Emily quickly answered, "The most famous bear in the world is *Smokey Bear.*"

"That's right," answered Papa. All the other kids moaned when they realized the answer was so simple, but they hadn't thought of it first.

Then, Rosalan spoke up, "Yes, but Smokey Bear is just a picture someone drew of a bear. He isn't real."

Beach Birthday

Papa smiled and said, "A lot of people think that, Rosalan. They think he is just a made up character used to remind people to be careful with fires in the forest. But, in fact, the real Smokey Bear was a little bear cub that forest rangers found clinging way up high in a burnt tree after the forest fire had been put out. That forest fire was right behind our log cabin ranch house, in the Capitan Mountains, back in New Mexico.

A careless traveler staying in the mountain pass right behind our ranch left a campfire burning. He just rode off on his horse not bothering to put the fire out, or throw water and dirt on it. It was in the summer time when there are a lot of dry leaves and sticks on the ground. A fire started and, in just a few minutes, the whole mountainside was ablaze. The animals that lived in the forest could sense the danger and began to run.

This little bear cub and his mother tried to get away, but found themselves trapped in the fire. The mother used her body to cover up her baby cub and save his life. After the fire was out, the little cub began to wander around looking for food. When he saw the forest rangers coming up the mountainside, he was scared, so he climbed to the top of a burnt pine tree and they found him clinging to the top of it crying.

The rangers couldn't help but feel sorry for the little cub, so they carefully climbed up the tree, and brought the little cub down to the ground. His little paws were burnt and charred from walking around in the hot embers left over from the fire. There was so much ash and soot on his fur coat that he looked like a smoky, grey bear not a little black bear. That's why the rangers named him Smokey Bear. They brought him back to the Ranger office and cleaned up his burns and fed him. He was just a tiny cub and not dangerous at all.

Smokey Bear

Everyone was taking pictures with Smokey Bear at the Ranger office and one of those pictures ended up at the newspaper office, along with the story of the brave rescue of Smokey Bear. Before long, the picture and the story spread across the nation until everyone heard of this famous bear. Smokey Bear became the symbol for being careful with fires in the forest.

At that point, the Forest Service in Washington, D.C. began using a drawing of Smokey Bear to remind people to be careful with fires. The real Smokey Bear lives in the Washington, D.C. Zoo now, safe and protected. Millions of people have come to see him, so he is the most famous bear in the world, and he came from right behind our New Mexico ranch house.

"How many of you kids have heard of Smokey Bear?" Around the fire, every hand went up. Papa wasn't surprised. Papa always had lots of stories and the children loved to listen to his tales of adventure and life on the wide-open range of New Mexico.

The next few weeks were wonderful for Pansy. She loved her new friends on N ½ Avenue and she loved the overnight camping on the beach. It was hard to say which she was enjoying more. Pansy could have never imagined that this trip would become so interesting and full of things to learn and see. Papa was right when he said, "It will be even better than school for this year." Pansy was feeling so happy; she would have never expected what was about to happen next.

Chapter 17

The Dream

The splash of the incoming *tide* crashing against the rocks and sand worked like an alarm clock to awaken the family. Pansy rolled over and peered out of her tent toward the ocean shore. A gentle ocean breeze crept through the opening in her tent and blew softly against her face. It would be nice to sleep a little longer she thought to herself. Then she remembered what day it was. The tide was coming in and Papa would be getting ready to catch crabs.

Pansy popped out of her sleeping bag and poked her head out of the tent. Sure enough, there was Papa getting the nets ready to go *"crabbing"* along the shore. Crabbing was fun. The little critters are easy to spot in the shallow water. Sometimes you can catch them with your bare hands, but Pansy learned that you have to be careful, because crabs have very powerful claws that really hurt when they pinch. The nets make it easier.

Papa was finishing up when Pansy walked out of the tent. "Are you ready to go crabbing, Pansy?" asked Papa.

"Yes, Papa," answered Pansy.

The sun was up, just over the watery horizon, so it would be easy to see the crabs moving in the shallow waters. They had already found the best crabbing spot on the Island, just a short walk from the campsite. It was a little place where the water spilled over onto the beach and made a little pool way back in the sand near the road when the tide was in. The little pool was often filled with so many crabs, all you had to do was swoop down with your net to snag two or three at a time.

As they walked along toward their crabbing spot, Papa asked Pansy if she was enjoying the Island. Pansy responded, "Oh, Papa, this was the best idea you ever had. I love being here. We get to eat all the crab and shrimp and fish we want. I get to splash in the salt water when I get hot and enjoy the ocean breeze every night. We sit around the campfire and I get to listen to the stories told by you and Mama. Then, there are all the kids to play with who live near the Big House. It is wonderful!"

Papa smiled and said to Pansy, "I'm glad you're having fun. I wanted this trip to be a wonderful experience for you."

"Tell me though, Pansy, are you ever homesick and ready to go back to the log cabin ranch house?"

Pansy didn't have to think long to answer. "Sometimes I wonder how everything is back home and I miss just sitting on the porch with you and Mama."

Papa smiled at Pansy saying . . ."I just wondered."

For an hour or more, they chased and caught crabs. Today wasn't as easy as other times; they really had to work to get enough crabs for a good meal. Papa never caught more crabs than the family could eat in one meal because, if the crabs die before you cook them, they can make you sick. Papa always knew things like that. Pansy thought it was because he was so smart, but Papa always said it was because he had learned by doing so many things wrong the first time. Then he would laugh.

As night fell over the Island, Papa had the campfire popping and everyone gathered around. Mama had prepared a surprise pie while they were gone crabbing earlier in the day. They sat around the fire, eating pie and drinking coffee. Pansy had water with a fresh lemon squeezed into it and a little sugar. It was story time and Papa was in the right mood to tell a good one.

"Pansy, have we ever told you about your Aunt Virginia and the miracle rocks?"

Pansy thought and said, "No, I don't think so. The last story you told me was about Uncle Will dying and then coming back from heaven to tell everyone what it was like."

"Well," Papa went on, "This story happened a few years after your Uncle Will died. The whole country was in a bad drought and there was not much money. Most people were so poor and they had no food. The government created places in many of the towns where people could get a bowl of soup."

"A bowl of soup?" Asked Pansy.

"Yes, Pansy," Papa continued, "These were called soup lines. Hundreds and, sometimes, thousands of people would line up for hours just to get a simple bowl of soup. Many people were losing their houses to the banks because they couldn't pay their loans anymore. The whole country was in very bad shape.

Now, all of this affected your Aunt Virginia and her family, too. The drought made it impossible to raise crops, which meant there was no money to pay for the farm, buy groceries, clothes, or anything else."

"So what did they do, Papa? "Pansy asked.

"They did what they always did," said Papa.

"Pray?" Pansy said, answering the question.

"Yes," said Papa, as he continued the story.

"Aunt Virginia gathered her family all around the kitchen table and they prayed. First of all, Virginia reminded the family that God promises in His Word that He would never leave us nor forsake us. Second, she reminded them that when their Papa died, he assured them that God would be right there with them, no matter what happened. Then, they prayed that God would be with them and supply their needs. All of this was done before they ate their next meal of *mush*. After the meal, everyone went to bed and no more was said about the hard times they were going through. Years later, her children recalled that they went through hard times and sometimes they had to eat mush, but they never went hungry."

Papa continued with the story. "The next day, about the middle of the morning, there came a knock at Virginia's front door. When Virginia came to the door, there was a man standing there who introduced himself as a government project manager. Now, Virginia had no idea who this man was or what a government project manager was doing at her door. After introducing himself to Virginia, he told her the government was building a gravel road a few miles from her farm and he had noticed some of her land was very rocky.

'Oh, yes,' said Virginia, 'Especially along the creek. None of that land is good for farming. It has too many rocks on it.'

'Well, Mrs. Rule, that's exactly why I am visiting with you. We need more rocks for this road and you need those rocks cleared off your land. Would you allow us to remove the rocks to use for the road and that will give you fresh, clear land to use for planting when this drought ends?'

Virginia eagerly said, 'Yes, I will accept the offer.' She knew this would give her more farmland and, eventually, more money in the future."

Papa continued, "For the next few weeks, trucks and tractors came in and out of the farm property hauling away thousands of pounds of rocks and clearing the rocky land behind the house and along the creek. Then one day, after several weeks, there was another knock at the door. The same man returned to see Virginia. She welcomed him into the living room and they sat down.

'We are finished, Mrs. Rule,' said the government project manager.

'Finished?' Virginia asked.

'Yes, we've taken all the rocks we needed for the gravel road. I think you'll find you have a lot more land to farm now than you did before,' he said.

Virginia smiled from ear to ear and thanked the man. Then, he reached into his pocket, and pulled out an envelope, handing it to Virginia.

'What is this?' she asked.

'Why, it's payment for your rocks, Ma'am,' said the government manager.

'Payment? For the rocks? I didn't expect to get paid,' said Virginia.

'Oh no, Mrs. Rule, we have to pay you for those rocks,' he answered.

Virginia opened the sealed envelope and slowly unfolded the check revealing the amount of five thousand dollars. This was a fortune. It was enough money to see them through the hard times and beyond. Virginia looked to heaven and thanked God right there and then."

Papa stopped and took a bite of his pie and another sip of his coffee. "What do you think of that story, Pansy?"

"It's amazing," she replied. "It seems like, no matter what happens to Aunt Virginia, she has learned to turn it over to God and trust Him to take care of things. Everything seems to always turn out right."

"Well, Pansy," said Papa. "It's not that everything was easy. As you know, Virginia suffered many losses and disappointments in the course of her life, but she never lost faith that God would see her through no matter what happened!"

Mama spoke up saying… "It's a good way for all of us to live our lives. I mean, trusting God to take care of us."

Papa quietly nodded in agreement, taking another sip of his coffee.

"Now," said Mama. "Guess what time it is?"

"Bedtime," said Pansy with less than an enthusiastic tone in her voice.

As Pansy closed her eyes and drifted off to sleep, she felt secure and safe. All these stories from her great-great grandmother being stolen by the Indians to this latest one about how God provided for her Aunt Virginia, even when so many others were hurting and hungry, caused her to know that no matter what happened, God would always be there for her if she called upon Him. She felt safe as she thought of all these things and safe because Star was curled up on his Indian rug right next to her bed.

On the other side of the wagon, Papa and Mama were sleeping too. Papa's sleep, however, was not so restful. He was tossing and turning from side to side. Deep in his sleep, he was dreaming of the ocean. He saw the waves so beautiful and calm with sea gulls and other sea birds, sitting on the water bobbing up and down with the gentle waves.

Then, in his dream, the birds began to rise up out of the water and fly quickly toward land. The sound of their voices was like a loud, screeching alarm. They all rose up at the same time and, as they flew swiftly to land, they kept looking back at the water. Then, in Papa's dream he saw what had alarmed the birds. A wave, a huge wave was speeding toward the shore and, behind the wave, there were ominous storm clouds and powerful winds. The closer the wave came, the higher it grew. As it neared the shore, it cast a long, dark, ominous shadow over the whole Island.

Papa saw people running back and forth, trying to get away from the wave, but by then, it was too late. The wave crashed on the shore, crushing everything in its path, and water covered the entire Island. Finally, Papa saw only water where the Island once had stood. All of the birds were desperately looking for a place to land. He woke up breathing hard as though he had been running for his life. He jumped up so fast that he awoke Mama too.

"What's the matter," asked Mama?

"We've got to leave," stated Papa! "We've got to leave right away. Something bad is coming to this Island, possibly a bad storm or something even worse. First thing in the morning, we must pack and head back home."

"Okay," said Mama, "Whatever you say but, right now, lay back down and go to sleep."

Papa lay down, but he could not sleep, as he kept thinking about all those people, helplessly, drowning under that water in his dream.

Chapter 18

The Road Home

Pansy awoke to the sound of boxes being packed and Mama's cast iron stove being set back on the wagon. When Pansy walked out of her tent, Mama quickly told her, "We are packing to head home." This came as a surprise, but it really didn't bother Pansy too much. She was ready to see the old log cabin ranch house again. What she heard next did bother her.

She could hear Papa visiting with some of the fellow campers. Pansy had rarely seen Papa's face as serious as it was that morning. Some of the men had gathered around him and he was telling them of the dream he had and trying to warn them to get off the Island. One man laughed at him and left. The others, about five or six men, stayed to listen. In the end, only Big Jim, who had become friends with Papa, gave any serious thought to leaving.

All of this grown up talk was making Pansy nervous inside. She never liked it when grown people go off and whisper to one another in order to keep the kids from knowing what was going on. Didn't they know that was worse than being told the truth could ever be? Pansy knew, though, when it was better to leave things alone and just say nothing for a while. This looked like one of those times.

After packing up on the beach, they went back to the Big House and loaded up the few personal items there. Then, they headed to Mr. Moore's store. Papa was in the store for what seemed like a very long time. He was returning the key to the house. Later, she would learn that he also was trying to warn Mr. Moore of his dream, but Mr. Moore just kept saying, "George, we have lived here all our lives and have seen many hurricanes blow through. They do a lot of damage but we've always survived just fine."

"Papa thanked Mr. Moore for the use of the house and returned his key. Pansy didn't really get to say goodbye to her friends, so she was busy writing a letter to Annie for all the kids in the neighborhood. She shared how much she loved the few weeks they had as friends and hoped that, one day, they might see each other again, even though Pansy knew that was unlikely. By noon, they were pulling out of Galveston and headed back to New Mexico.

The trip back through town and across the bridge was not nearly as eventful as when they first arrived. For Pansy, the day was both a little bit sad and a little bit happy, maybe even just a tiny exciting. She thought to herself, there are still many miles ahead and who knows what we might see or what might happen! With that, she jumped off the pillows at the back of the wagon and ran up to where Papa was leading the horses.

"Papa," she said, "Thank you for taking us on this trip. Papa . . . I love you." Papa put his big arm around her little body and pulled her next to him real close. "You guide the horses," he said, as he handed Pansy the reigns. "I'm tired and I want to rest awhile."

Pansy's hands gripped the reigns tightly as they bumped along the road leading off of the Island bridge and toward the west. By now, the sun was high overhead and the day was becoming warm.

Pansy thought about how difficult it might be to sleep tonight on those old spring mattresses, after living in the house on N ½ Avenue for the last three months. N ½ Avenue! "Oh no," she thought to herself. "What about Papa's dream and all of my friends?"

"Papa!" Pansy spoke with alarm in her voice.

Papa jumped, as he awoke, and said, "What's wrong?"

Papa grabbed for the reigns and Pansy surrendered them to him. "What's going to happen to all my friends on N ½ Avenue? We should have stayed and warned them!" cried Pansy.

Papa looked down at his daughter, with caring eyes, and put his arm around her again. Papa spoke to her in a gentle voice. "Pansy, the warning was for us. God told me to get off the Island and so that's just what we are doing. You saw the reaction of the men to whom I was talking. Most of them just ignored me or laughed it off. God will have to speak to their hearts as he did mine."

Pansy seemed distressed with this answer. She spoke back to Papa. "We should go back and warn everyone or at least our friends on N ½ Avenue."

Papa paused before he spoke, but then responded to her, saying "Pansy, a wise old deacon in the church once told me 'God will put your mail in your mail box.'"

"What's that mean?" Pansy asked.

"It means that God deals with every man individually. He will have to warn others to get off that Island or protect them from the darkness that's coming. All the warning in the world will mostly go unheeded."

"You mean there is nothing we can do?" Pansy said, nearly on the edge of tears.

"Oh no! I didn't say that. There is something very powerful and effective we can do," answered Papa.

"Oh, you mean pray," Pansy replied, with a tone of sadness mixed with unbelief in her voice.

Papa smiled at his young daughter. "What did you learn on that island when you were lost and stranded?"

Papa said this, with a knowing look on his face. Pansy quietly gave the answer she knew was true. "I learned that God really does hear our prayers."

Papa smiled, and said, "Right! If it was true on "Tucker Island," then it's true as we travel along this dusty trail . . . right?"

Pansy looked up, knowing Papa was right, but, nevertheless, wanting to do something more than pray.

"I'll tell you what, Pansy, let's agree to pray every night for the people of Galveston Island and, for whatever is coming, that God will help them and be with them... okay?"

Pansy looked back at her papa. "Okay," she agreed. The two of them sat on the bench of the wagon for a while, each lost in their own thoughts.

Then, Papa spoke up and said. "Pansy, did I ever tell you about the city man who showed up at the ranch one day?"

Pansy thought for a moment, and then replied, "No, I don't remember that story."

Papa began. "There was this man from the big city. Someplace like Chicago, I think. He came out to visit his cousin in Lincoln. Now, this cousin lived down the road a piece from us, but not too far. One day, I saw this city man strolling down the main road in front of the house, so I said 'hello' to him and he answered back. He was a right friendly man.

As I remember, he was a little overdressed for the prairie. He was all gussied up with a suit and tie and a matching vest. He looked more like a man going to a wedding than one out for a walk. So, I said to him, 'Sir, where are you headed this morning?'

Papa and the City Man

'Lincoln!' He answered.

I am sure I had a strange look on my face when I said to him, 'Lincoln, Sir? Why that's a half day's ride by horse through the Lincoln Pass.'

'I don't intend to use the road going through the pass. I plan to take a shortcut over the mountain,' he said in a determined voice.

'Over the mountain?' I know I sounded pretty strong with my response, but I thought this man was out of his mind.

I knew he didn't know the country and he didn't realize that Capitan Peak is over 10,000 feet high. I was worried he would get lost or injured or, worse yet, attacked by some wild animal."

Papa continued, "Pansy, I spent the better part of a half hour trying to convince that city man that this was a really bad idea. I even offered to take him into Lincoln, but after all my talking, he turned toward that mountain top and began to walk as though I had never said a word."

"So what happened to him, Papa?" Pansy questioned anxiously.

Papa shook his head and answered. "What happened? Just exactly what I thought would happen. After about two days, his cousin came by asking if I had seen him. I told him what I just told you and we both gathered up our ranch hands and twelve of us headed up into the mountain looking for this *yayhoo*."

Pansy interrupted "Did you find him?"

"We sure did." Papa said. "Three days later, half starved, and freezing from the cold mountain air. He had wandered around in circles until he didn't know which direction he was going. He would have died if we hadn't found him in time."

Pansy thought for a minute then said, "Papa, that man was not very smart, was he?"

Papa smiled and spoke again. "No, Pansy, he was as smart as any man, maybe smarter, but he didn't understand the land he was in.

He didn't understand how dangerous the mountains could be or how things, which look close in the mountains, can be miles and miles away."

Papa continued, "No, Pansy, he was plenty smart, but he was stubborn and didn't want to admit that he might be wrong or that he might not know something someone else, like me, might know. His stubbornness almost cost him his life. So, you see, we just need to pray for the people of Galveston that God will protect them and be with them. We need to pray that God will speak to their hearts, just like He spoke to mine."

"Okay," said Pansy "I see what you are saying. It was the man's stubbornness that got in the way of him being able to hear what you had to say."

That is just the same as when our stubbornness can get in the way of hearing God or His word." Papa smiled. "Pansy, you're a smart girl!"

Pansy jumped down from the slow moving wagon and began to walk next to Star. Star kept close watch over her as they walked along. Pansy was still concerned about her friends back in Galveston, but it made her feel better to know she could pray for their safety. Occasionally, she would throw a stick for Star to fetch. She thought to herself how Star never tired of the same game over and over.

The family camped that night near the small town of Alvin, Texas, which was several miles away from the ocean. Papa wanted to get as far away from the water as possible that first night, so they kept traveling down the road, even past dark. There were no community campgrounds, so Papa just found a good spot under some tallow trees and made camp. Papa set up camp quickly always checking for snakes first, since San Antonio. Because it was so late, dinner consisted of things Mama could scrape together without cooking. There was cornmeal bread from breakfast and some dried beef. These would have to do until tomorrow.

Pansy climbed into her bed and pulled the covers up under her chin. Then, she heard Papa's voice in her ear, saying, "Aren't you forgetting something? We need to pray."

Pansy climbed down and Papa, Mama, and Pansy joined hands, in a little circle, to pray. First, they thanked God for bringing them safely this far on their journey and for blessing them with food and supplies. Then, they asked God to keep them safe as they traveled on. Finally, they prayed for the people of Galveston Island. They asked God to spare them and help many to escape the coming darkness. Papa always called it darkness, because he couldn't be certain what horrible thing was coming, but he was certain in his heart that he needed to get away. For the next several weeks, as they traveled home, this would be their nightly prayer.

After prayer, Mama walked with Pansy back to her bunk on the side of the wagon. Just as Pansy was about to climb up, Mama moaned "Ohhh!" Pansy turned and looked, but before she could say another word, Mama said again, "Ohhh!"

"What is it?" questioned Pansy.

Mama smiled at Pansy and said, "The baby is kicking me. Do you want to feel it?"

Pansy reached her hand toward Mama's growing stomach to feel the thumping of the baby against Mama's tummy. Mama smiled, and said, "It's definitely in there."

Pansy smiled back and said, "You mean, she is definitely in there!"

This had become a little game Mama and Pansy played. Pansy knew that the baby could just as easily be a boy, but she was wishing, hoping, and praying for a girl. At the end of the game, Mama would always say, "Just so it's healthy!"

"So, how soon will the baby be here?" questioned Pansy, as she lay her head back down on the pillow.

"I think about four more weeks, maybe five," responded Mama.

Pansy thought for a moment, then said, "but will we be back home by then?"

"Probably not," replied Mama.

"What will we do if the baby comes when we're still traveling? How will you be able to have the baby on the road?" Pansy spoke in worried tones.

Mama answered softly. "Pansy, don't you worry. Babies are born every day. It's a natural part of life. When the time gets close, though, Papa will find a good place to settle for a couple weeks. I'll have the baby and, when I am strong enough, we'll move on back home. Okay?"

Pansy looked at her Mama's soft face and loving eyes. The moon was shining bright and it lit up her hair with moonlight. It was a picture she would treasure forever. "Okay, Mama." Pansy replied. Then, she drifted off to sleep.

Chapter 19

The Reunion

A few days later, the Hunt family had pushed on to the west many miles. When they crossed the wide Brazos River, Papa told everyone that the real trip home had begun. He told them that the Brazos River separated the east from the west in Texas and, now, they were heading toward the wilderness area of the south.

"There will be lots of cactus and sand, and not much water, so we'll have to keep stocked up on supplies every chance we get." He said.

Pansy asked, "What kind of things can we expect to see, Papa?"

"Well, Pansy, as we travel West we're going to come to Del Rio. That's *Roy Bean country.*"

Pansy had a confused look on her face. "What are Roy beans?" She asked.

Papa laughed so hard, he almost fell off the side of the wagon. "No child . . . Roy Bean isn't something you eat; it is a man by the name of Roy, and his last name is Bean. For many years, he has been the only Law west of the Pecos River. He's a Lawman and a Judge."

Pansy snarled up her face and said, "He has a funny name, anyway."

"I guess you're right, Pansy. I'll bet more than one of the bad guys he's put on trial would have liked to eat him up like a bean."

"Anyway," Papa continued, "When we get to Del Rio, we will catch up with the Pecos River. It will lead us into New Mexico, then up into the mountains and home."

Home! Just the sound of the word felt good to hear. The trip had been wonderful but, to Pansy, her home was the log cabin ranch house, and she was beginning to get anxious to get back.

"So, are you ready to go home?" asked Papa.

"I sure am!" replied Pansy and, from the back of the wagon, Mama sounded out an even louder, "Yes, Sir!!!"

Papa laughed and said, "Then I suppose you're not interested in a stop through the town of Chesterville?"

Pansy's eyes shot wide open, "You mean the town where my friend, Ginny, lives?" Pansy's voice was filled with excitement and anticipation. Papa smiled and shook his head "yes."

Pansy began to talk a thousand miles an hour, asking Mama if she heard what Papa said, and then asked, "Will Ginny be there? How far is it? How long can we stay?" On and on she went. Papa said she was like a bucking bronco let out of a cage. She just couldn't stop.

It turned out that, both Papa and Mama, knew the stop was planned long ago with the Morgan's way back when they parted ways on the trail to Galveston. Mrs. Morgan had told Mama they could stay for a few weeks at their home to have the baby if it worked out. Mama had written Mrs. Morgan a few days before they left Galveston to let her know they would be leaving in a few weeks. Then, after Papa's dream, they left the Island earlier than expected. Mama didn't think they would stay to have the baby, but they still wanted to see the Morgan's on the way home.

Pansy was so thrilled. She jumped off the wagon and ran around it three times, with Star chasing her like she was a rabbit. Finally, Papa told her to stop before she spooked the horses. Pansy climbed back into the wagon and said to Papa, "So, how long till we get to Ginny's town?" Papa grinned from ear to ear and announced, "Next stop, Chesterville!"

As the family rolled into the outskirts of the town of Chesterville, Texas, they could see all kinds of activity. Brightly colored wagons lined the streets on the edge of town. Many of the wagons were hauling horses and other animals like bulls and longhorn steers. At first, the family wondered what this could be, but then they saw painted on the side of one of the big wagons in bright colors **BUFFALO BILL'S WILD WEST SHOW.** When Pansy saw the sign, she remembered Ginny said that her uncle rode a horse and did tricks in the show.

"I'll bet Ginny is excited to see her uncle in the show," Pansy exclaimed.

Papa pointed out that it looked as though the show was being set up near the edge of town. On down the road, they traveled past the show and past the little houses at the edge of town until they came to the center of the city.

It was a small town, but big enough to have some of the latest things, like motorcars and streetlights. In the very center of the town was a large, brick courthouse with a steeple that reached up so high it made Pansy dizzy. The courthouse was built on a square with streets on all four sides and little shops lining the sidewalks. All the buildings looked clean and new in the town. A few shoppers were moving from store to store but, it was late in the day, and most shops were beginning to close. Pansy spotted a grocery store and a meat market. On the other side of the square she saw a barbershop, but it looked closed for the day, and a candy and ice cream parlor.

"Oh, no, Pansy," Mama spoke up. "We're heading for the Morgan's house." Pansy sort of laughed that Mama could read her mind so well.

Then, Mama spoke again, giving a little hope to her daughter. "Maybe tomorrow." Pansy smiled.

Papa turned the wagon off of the city square when he spotted Fourth Street. "This is it," announced Papa. "The Morgan's live on Fourth Street."

The street was lined with tall oak trees that stretched to heaven. Two and three story houses rose like magnificent mountains on both sides. Each house had a yard in front and back with green grass and colorful flowers. Nearly every home had a white picket fence surrounding the front yard and leading to a sidewalk where Pansy saw children here and there running up and down, riding bicycles and playing games like jacks and pick-up sticks. She saw girls jumping rope and boys running and making noise, as boys will. Pansy was so taken with the pleasant view from the bench seat of the wagon, she hardly noticed when Papa began to slow the horses and move the wagon over next to the curb.

"We are here!" Papa announced.

Pansy snapped out of her dream state, realizing that she was parked in front of the Morgan's home. It was the largest, most beautiful Victorian style home she had ever seen. She realized, at once, that the dollhouse Ginny's dad had made for her was a replica of the very house in which she lived.

It was painted brightly in white with colorful blues and yellows on the trim. It was three stories high, with a huge porch on the front that held an enormous swing. It looked like the largest house on the block and, by far, the most beautiful. Mr. Morgan built houses for a living so he wanted his own home to be like a showplace to demonstrate his skill as a craftsman in wood.

The family had no more than climbed down from the wagon when the front door of the house swung wide open and a smiling Ginny came bounding across the porch and down the steps. Pansy spotted her and, in a moment, the two girls were hugging and bouncing up and down.

Closely behind, came Mrs. Morgan with a broad smile on her face. The mothers met at the sidewalk and immediately began talking about the baby. Mrs. Morgan told Papa that Mr. Morgan would be home soon.

"I just had a feeling you might show up today." Mrs. Morgan said. Everyone moved into the house and the reunion of the Hunt and Morgan families began.

That evening, all six of the friends sat around the Morgan's enormous dinner table and gave thanks to God over a wonderful meal of chicken and dumplings made by Mrs. Morgan, herself, with a little help from Mama. Pansy and Ginny chattered like two clucking hens, while the grown-ups talked of bigger things, like the Nation and the weather, and Papa's dark dream about Galveston. The Morgan's agreed that they would be in prayer for the people of Galveston, too.

"How long can you stay with us?" asked Mr. Morgan.

"Only a day or two." replied Papa.

Mr. Morgan spoke again, "Oh, George, I do wish you could stay longer than that!"

Ginny's mom said "I wish you would just stay with us until the baby is born." Papa and Mama both shook their heads and answered, almost in unison, "No, No… that would be too long. This baby is not coming for a month yet."

One more time, Mr. Morgan spoke up. "You are welcome to stay. Our house is your house for as long as you need it."

"That's kind of you," Papa replied, "but we do need to press on toward home soon. Thank you for your offer, but we'll be going in a couple days."

No more was said of staying, except Mr. Morgan mentioned how he wished they would stay for the big show coming to town on Saturday. "It's Buffalo Bill's Wild West Show. Ginny's uncle is part of it."

"We saw the wagons as we were riding into town," said Papa.

"Yes." Mr. Morgan answered back. "We're celebrating the completion of the railroad coming to the city. The railroad is going to really make this town boom. It will be good for all the merchants and, certainly, good for my business. More people, more houses!"

Papa smiled and nodded in agreement. Papa was happy for his friend but, as for himself, he would rather live free and away from large crowds. Happiness for Papa was the wide-open range where the nearest neighbor was a mile or two away. He was missing home and anxious to get back. Nevertheless, Papa agreed, to the girls' great happiness, that the family would stay until Saturday so they could go to Buffalo Bill's Wild West Show and meet Ginny's uncle.

It was as though the girls had not been apart a day. They went right back to playing with the games and toys they played with on the road. There were, however, many more dolls in Ginny's room. She had more toys, dolls, and games than Pansy could ever imagine. Three days flew by, as though they were a moment, and Saturday was here. The girls rose early, got dressed, and ready for the big day at the Wild West Show.

"Everybody in town will be there." Ginny told Pansy. "You'll get to meet some of my friends.

Buffalo Bill's Wild West Show traveled to hundreds of cities and small towns during those days. The show featured cowboys and sharp shooters doing all sorts of amazing tricks on their horses and displaying expert skills with guns. The show was, more or less, the last remaining part of the Wild West.

As part of the show, the cowboys, who were more like actors, would pretend to chase a bad guy who would be doing all sorts of tricks from the back of his horse, trying to get away. The good guys would rope him or pretend to shoot him. There were also clowns and other acts, plus booths where you could test your own skills at shooting against that of the experts, for a nickel. The show was a lot of fun and, Ginny was right, the entire community came out to join the festivities.

The two families arrived early and were among the first to find their seats in the stands. Some of the cowboys were warming up in the arena, including Ginny's Uncle Frank. When he rode near them, Ginny waved and hollered, "Hi, Uncle Frank!" as loud as she could. The man on the horse swung around and rode right up to them. Sitting on his horse, Uncle Frank was just even with the grandstand so he was able to reach across and shake hands with everyone.

Mr. Morgan introduced Frank to Papa, Mama, and Pansy. Frank tipped his hat to Mama and hugged his sister, Mrs. Morgan. Then, he reached out and plucked Ginny off of her feet and onto his horse. No sooner had she landed on the horse, than he plucked Pansy up and set her in front of Ginny. The three of them rounded the arena, waving, and greeting the other cowboys.

On the other side of the arena, Frank stopped and talked to a couple cowboys. The three men all rode back to the grandstands with the two girls. When they arrived back at the stand, Frank spoke first, as he passed the girls back over to their mothers.

"Gentlemen, I would like you to meet the star of this show and the greatest horseman in the country, Mr. William Cody, better known as Buffalo Bill."

Frank went on with his introduction. "And this, Gentleman, is Mr. Bill Hickok, sometimes known as Wild Bill Hickok."

When Papa shook hands with Mr. Cody, he greeted him and said, "Hello, Sir, my name is George Alonzo Hunt. My father has told me many incredible stories about you both." *Cody and Hickok* both looked at each other with surprise, as did the Morgan's and even Pansy.

Mr. Cody lifted up the brim of his hat and said, "Do you mean to say that your father is *Alonzo Hunt*?" All eyes kept going back and forth listening to this unexpected exchange.

Hickok spoke next, "Your father and the two of us served as army scouts in Kansas after the war. The last time I remember seeing Alonzo, we were playing cards in a saloon down in Coffeyville. How is your father?"

"You wouldn't believe it, Gentlemen," Papa said to the men. "He lives on a farm in Bedford, Iowa, and still does cartwheels every day to stay in shape."

Buffalo Bill laughed and said, "Cartwheels, I'd forgotten about that. He always loved to do those at the most unnatural times. Your father was a great soldier and a great storyteller. When you see him again, tell him we said, 'hello!' I hope you enjoy the show, folks. I've got to go now." Hickok and Cody rode off along with Frank. The Morgan's and the girls were standing with their mouths open in shock.

Finally, Mr. Morgan spoke up. "So, I talked you into staying until Saturday so you can meet my brother-in-law, Frank, who rides in the show, and you don't bother telling me that your father was best friends with the owner of the show." Papa just smiled.

The show was wonderful. The cowboys did unbelievable tricks from their horses and with their guns. The acting was exciting and sometimes funny. The horses were beautiful and could perform all kinds of skills. Even Papa, who wasn't one to put much stock in shows or performances, had to admit it was spectacular.

At one point in the show, after shooting a perfect bull's eye fifty feet away from the back of a moving horse, Uncle Frank grabbed the paper target and trotted around the stands so everyone could see the hole in the target. He then gave the target to his niece, Ginny, and she gave him a kiss over the rail of the stand. Everyone applauded. Pansy could not think of a more thrilling day. However, all the fun could not have prepared the girls for what was about to happen next.

When the show was over, the girls asked if they could go walk around the displays and meet some of Ginny's friends. They were given permission and told to be back at the house by five o'clock. Each girl had a few coins in her purse for riding the ponies and getting some candy. Together, they walked along and looked at the carnival booths next to the Wild West Show. Ginny ran into some of her friends and introduced them to Pansy. The friends were on their way to join some other kids on the edge of town about five minutes away. Pansy didn't think anything of it, but walked along with Ginny.

As they walked, Pansy noticed something odd about Ginny. When she was with her friends she didn't sound or talk the same. She acted more like someone else, instead of the way she was on the road or in her house. Their feet carried them swiftly to the rest of the group who had gathered on the edge of town. There were six children plus Pansy. It was a mix of boys and girls, but two boys, Patrick and Chad were doing most of the talking, and Pansy could see, in a minute, that whatever these two said, no one was going to disagree with them.

Patrick was a big muscular boy and Chad was, unusually short, with curly, unkempt black hair. When the girls arrived, the boys were bragging about how they could do a lot of those tricks the cowboys were doing in the show and how those things aren't so hard if you have all day to practice.

Then Patrick spoke up and said, "Chad and I found a cave on the other side of town behind the old fruit tree orchard."

One of the other guys spoke up, "There's no caves around here!"

Patrick responded, "It's more of a mine but it's like a cave. Who wants to go check it out?" Some hands slowly rose, including Ginny's to Pansy's surprise.

Again, Patrick spoke up, "What's the matter with the rest of you? Are you chicken?" At this challenge, the rest of the hands slowly went up in the air, all except Pansy's hand.

"Let's go!" shouted Patrick and they all began to move.

Pansy grabbed Ginny by the arm and said, "No, Ginny, you're not really going, are you?"

Ginny snapped back at Pansy, "Stop it, Pansy, you're going to make me look foolish in front of my friends."

Again, Pansy tried to persuade Ginny that this didn't look like a good idea. "I don't want to embarrass you but an old mine is not a safe place. Something bad could occur and no one would know where you are or what happened."

This time Ginny said "Come on, Pansy, it will be fun. If you're my friend, you'll come with me."

At this point, the leader, Patrick, could hear the girls disagreeing, so he stopped and spoke to Pansy. "Hey, new girl, what's your name?"

Ginny answered, "This is my friend, Pansy. I think she's just a little scared."

Patrick spoke saying, "Come on, don't worry, I've done this lots of times. We will be back before the sun sets." Terror ran through Pansy's heart. Those were the exact same words Little Joe had said to her before she climbed into that boat and became stranded on Tucker Island.

"No! I won't go!" Pansy stopped moving and set her jaw as if she were ready to fight.

In that moment, she realized how much older and wiser she had become since that day in the boat with Little Joe. She wasn't going to make that mistake twice. She turned and walked away, back in the direction of the Wild West Show. Ginny came a few steps her way, begging her to come back, assuring her that everything would be okay. Pansy kept walking. Had she turned around, she would have seen

Ginny, looking back and forth from her group of friends, then back to Pansy, trying to decide what to do. Finally, she joined her friends shouting back to Pansy, "Don't tell my parents where I am."

As Pansy walked on, she could hear the group shouting, "Chicken!" toward her and laughing as they walked away. They couldn't see the tears forming in her eyes and rolling down her cheeks as she shuffled along. How could a day begin so perfect and so happy, then turn so awful this fast? Pansy knew she was doing the right thing but that didn't make it hurt any less.

"Now, what should I do?" Pansy thought to herself. "I can hang out here at the show until she comes back or I can tell Papa and Mama what's going on. If I do that, Ginny will hate me, but what if something horrible happens in that mine, I'll hate myself for not telling." Pansy wandered around for about ten minutes until it became clear as a cup of water what she had to do.

She had to tell her parents what had happened. Pansy made her way along the main street of town, back toward the center square, then on to Fourth Street. By the time she got back to the house, half an hour had gone by. She stood at the bottom of the stairs leading to the front door. For a moment she hesitated, then slowly walked up the steps and entered the front door.

Meanwhile, the group had arrived at the mine or, as Patrick liked to call it, the "cave of darkness."

"Come on guys, let's go in!" With that, Patrick bent down and walked into the dark tunnel. He had brought an oil lantern for light. Obediently, the others followed. First, Chad, then Ginny, and another girl followed behind the last two. Into the cave of darkness, they slowly walked along. There was a musty smell in the place with old tools and machinery scattered here and there.

For years, the old mine had been sealed up and covered in weeds, but Patrick and Chad discovered it one morning a couple days earlier when they were chasing some rabbits. The old door had rusted away and it didn't take much to pull it off, revealing the dark entrance to the mine. At the time, neither Patrick nor Chad had a lantern for light so they didn't go inside very far. What the other children did not understand was both Patrick and Chad were too scared to explore the mine alone so they pressured the little group to come with them.

Into the mine they pushed ahead, with Patrick, as their leader, who was driven by his own need to be seen as tough and invincible. Patrick led the little group down the shaft and into an area where the boards, holding up the roof, had become weak from years of stress. They heard the sound of creaking boards above their heads and, with that, two of the stragglers turned around and headed back toward the opening.

"We're out of here," they announced.

Patrick turned toward them and was about to holler, "Chickens!" when a second sound was heard and the snapping of timbers.

Meanwhile, back at the house, Pansy was explaining, "So, I don't know where they are right now, but I know they were headed toward that mine shaft!" Pansy had just finished explaining what had happened to her parents and the Morgan's.

Mr. Morgan rushed out of the house with George and Pansy right behind him. He started his motorcar and George jumped into the seat next to him while Pansy jumped in the back. On the way to the mine, they stopped by the fire station and gathered every man they could see walking along to come help.

By the time they arrived at the mine, they could see dust billowing out from the shaft like an explosion. Three children, all covered in dust from head to toe, were lying on the grass outside the opening. None of these three were Ginny.

Cave In

Mr. Morgan began to rush toward the opening, but George held him back, saying, "It's too dangerous. Let the firemen work to get them out."

Mr. Morgan began to holler into the opening for his daughter and kept listening for an answer. Over and over, he yelled her name but there was no response. Within minutes, the word had spread across the city.

Even some of the cowboys from the show came to help because they had experience working in mines. They knew how to secure the opening and the ceiling so that the rescue team would not become victims themselves. Slowly, they worked to remove the mountain of dirt that had fallen into the shaft of the mine.

Mama showed up with Mrs. Morgan. Within an hour, practically the whole town was there, including the parents of both Chad and Patrick. One of the ministers led the crowd in prayer, while mothers and fathers stood asking God to spare their children.

Pansy kept repeating the scripture, "I will never leave you nor forsake you." She kept praying that the same God who was with her on that island would be with Ginny and those boys in this cave.

The digging began around four o'clock in the afternoon. It was well past nine o'clock that evening when someone yelled out of the hole "We found them and they are alive!" Cheers erupted from the crowd.

Ginny was the first out, all covered with dirt, and suffering a broken leg. "I am so sorry, Mom." Ginny cried.

When she saw Pansy looking down on her, she broke into tears saying, "Oh, Pansy, you were right, you were right; I should have listened to you. Please forgive me."

Pansy rubbed her friend's forehead and said, "Ginny, I forgive you. I am just glad you're going to be okay."

Patrick and Chad were brought out next. Other than bruises, they were okay, but they had a lot of explaining to do to some very unhappy parents.

The day had seen the highest of highs and the lowest of lows. The day had also seen a town come together to save their children. Everyone agreed that Pansy's decision not to join her friends and to share the information with her parents probably helped save their children's lives because the rescue began almost immediately.

As Pansy laid her head on the pillow that night, she was thankful that she listened to what she knew in her heart to be right. She thought to herself, "God will never leave us or forsake us."

Chapter 20

Home At Last

Pansy was lying in bed, not yet asleep, when Papa opened the door, letting a shaft of light slide across the bed and over Pansy's face. Seeing her eyes still open, he walked into the room, with Mama behind him.

"Hey, Pansy, we have an agreement, remember?" Papa questioned with a pleasant look on his face. "We agreed to pray every night for the people of Galveston and I think we need to thank God for being with us today."

Pansy hopped out of bed and knelt down on her knees. Together, they prayed, as Papa had said, and then added a special prayer for Ginny to be okay in the hospital where she was recovering from her broken leg. Pansy also prayed for Chad and Patrick and all the other kids that were caught in the mineshaft. "Thank you, Lord, that everyone was rescued and saved from that horrible mine. Amen"

Pansy crawled back under the blankets, while her mama tucked her in. Papa sat down on the edge of the bed and said, "Pansy, I want you to know how proud I am of the way you handled the predicament in which you found yourself today. You could have gone along with Ginny and the other kids. Even when you decided not to follow them, you could have kept what they were about to do to yourself. That might have resulted in a much greater disaster than what actually did happen."

Pansy smiled at Papa and Mama.

Mama spoke up saying, "You reminded us of your Great-Great Grandmother Nancy Ross today."

Pansy looked puzzled and replied, "Really?"

"Yes, you did," Mama continued, "When you stood your ground and refused to go along at the insistence of everyone else, including your friend Ginny, you reminded me of the way Nancy stood tall, refusing to show fear, in front of the Indian tribe."

Then Papa added, "And, Pansy, when you kept walking away even when they were laughing at you and calling you names, it reminded me of running the gauntlet. Like your Great-Great Grandmother Nancy Ross, you just kept going and refused to be stopped by their attacks. We're both so proud of you."

Then, Pansy looked at her parents' faces, in the half moonlight filling the room, and thoughtfully asked, "But why did Ginny act that way? Why did she turn on me when she got around her friends?"

Papa rubbed his chin, the way he often did, when a story is about to begin. "You know, Pansy, I never told you the rest of the story about Aunt Virginia and Uncle Will when their house burned."

"Yes, you did," Pansy replied. "They got a brand new house given to them that fit perfectly on the old foundation."

Papa went on, "Well, yes, you are right, but that wasn't the only thing that happened to them that year." Pansy sat up in bed and her eyes were glued to Papa's words as though they were floating in front of her face.

Again, Papa spoke, "After the fire and bringing in the new house, they still had to get settled. They had lost everything in the fire. I mean literally everything, except the clothes on their backs. People around the community began to bring items to help them.

They brought clothes and furniture. The outpouring of love for Will and Virginia was so great that they finally asked people to stop bringing things because they had too much. At one point, they had seven new stoves donated to them. People just wouldn't stop blessing them."

Papa continued, "Will had a field full of wheat growing and thirty-seven hogs. Everything was looking wonderful, when disaster struck again. First, his hogs began to die."

"How come they died?" questioned Pansy.

Papa replied, "They got a disease called *cholera* and, one by one, all but five of them died. It was a disaster."

Soon, the wheat in the field was tall and ready for harvest, so they cut it down and piled it into three huge mountains of wheat to be threshed."

Pansy looked confused and said, "What is threshed?"

Papa answered, "Threshed is when you take the long stock of wheat and remove or separate the actual wheat grain from the stock. It takes a special and very expensive machine. Farmers would gather up their wheat into mountainous, high piles. A man with a *threshing machine* would come and separate the grain so it was ready to sell."

"Okay," Pansy replied, still wondering what any of this had to do with her friend, Ginny, turning on her.

Papa went on talking. "When the man came to Uncle Will's farm to thresh his wheat, he set the machine up, turned it on, and then went off to take care of some other business. While he was away, the machine broke down and began to throw fiery sparks everywhere. The sparks caught your Uncle Will's wheat on fire and it burned every bit of it."

"How awful!" Pansy exclaimed. "What did Uncle Will do?"

Papa looked very serious, as he went on with the story, saying, "Now, Pansy, this is the important part to learn from this story."

"When the man returned to discover his machine had burned up all of Will's wheat, he felt terrible. He was aware he should not have left the machine on while he was away, so he knew it was his fault. At the time, he thought it was okay, but now he understood the decision to leave was a mistake.

The man went to your Uncle Will and said, 'I have no money to pay you back for the wheat I burned up, so please take my machine in payment for your wheat.'

Now, Uncle Will knew this man had ten children and he used that machine to make a living and feed his family. Will could have taken the machine, fixed it up, and made even more money than his little wheat field would have produced."

Pansy interrupted Papa's story saying, "He didn't do that, did he? He forgave the man and trusted God to take care of everything, right?" Papa smiled.

"You are exactly right, Pansy!" Papa said, with a wide smile on his face.

"Uncle Will understood something very important," Papa continued. "When Will and Virginia's house burned down, God took care of them and replaced everything. They never knew for sure what caused the house to burn down, but Virginia always worried that she might have left a burning log in the oven. It didn't matter whose fault it was, God took care of them anyway. There was no way Will would take this man's machine for making a mistake. He forgave the man just as you said. That act of forgiveness caused people in the community to stop and think about their own lives. Many others came to know God as a result of the way Uncle Will handled the issue."

Papa's story was over. He looked at Pansy, waiting for her to speak. Pansy looked at her parents and said, "What you're saying is that I need to forgive Ginny for her mistake, just like you forgave me when I ran off to Tucker Island without telling anyone. We both made mistakes and we both need forgiveness."

Papa and Mama looked at each other in amazement, overjoyed at their daughter's ability to understand these deep spiritual lessons. Papa stood up with Mama. After two kisses, one on each of Pansy's cheeks, Papa announced, "Like I said, we are both very proud of you."

Dust was flying up from the wagon wheels as the family scooted along the trail at a slightly faster pace than they had been traveling. Mama was becoming more and more uncomfortable, bouncing in the wagon, almost nine months pregnant, and expecting the baby very soon. Papa had found the road following the Pecos River and was speeding toward a town he had found on the map called Hagerman, New Mexico.

Mama was spending most of her time on the pillows at the back of the wagon. Mrs. Morgan had donated a few extra pillows to make the journey more comfortable. The leisurely trip was over. Now, they were, like the horse headed for the barn, going as fast as Mama could stand the bouncing.

Papa told Mama that Hagerman was a nice town with a real doctor and they would have no problem finding a room to rent for a few days. Mama smiled and hoped her husband knew what he was talking about. Secretly, Papa was also hoping he knew what he was talking about. They covered 150 miles in three days, trying to get to Hagerman. When they crossed the line between Texas and New Mexico, there was a broken down old sign along the side of the road welcoming people to the Territory of New Mexico. The sign was rusty and laying on its side.

"Some welcome, huh, Pansy?" Papa laughed, and then drove the horses on down the dusty trail.

They arrived in Hagerman, New Mexico, well after dark. The only store open was a saloon and the sheriff's office. Papa went to see the sheriff, but there was a sign on the door telling people they would find the sheriff in the saloon. While Mama slept on the pillows in the back of the wagon, Pansy held the reigns and kept the team of horses steady. Papa found the sheriff in the saloon and was happy to learn there was a doctor in town and, in the morning, the family could probably find a room to rent.

The next morning, the family ate a warm breakfast at Rosa's Cantina, and then headed over to the doctor's house. Pansy stayed with the wagon while Papa and Mama went into the doctor's office. She kept busy, watching the horses and buggies moving up and down the street. Sitting next to her on the wagon seat was her best friend, Star.

"Are you ready to go home, Star?" Pansy asked. Star looked at her with that innocent look dogs seem to have. It was always hard for her to believe that this same dog, which was always so gentle and calm, could, in a moment's notice, rise up and fight mountain lions, rattle snakes, and even skunks. She had to laugh, when she realized, the only battle he ever lost was the one with the skunk.

Pansy sat back against the canvas of the wagon and thought of the whole trip from start to finish. Papa was right. This trip has been just as good of an education as going to school. She had met so many different people and learned so much from the stories and adventures along the way.

In fact, she was a year older, but she felt like she had grown up more than a year. She understood some things about herself and God, and now she had a much greater appreciation for her family and her history. It had been a good year and the best part was about to happen. She was about to get a baby "sister" she hoped.

Pansy was just thinking about these things when Mama, then Papa, stepped out of the doctor's house. The doctor stood on the porch with them, shaking hands for a moment, then he disappeared into the house, and the family was soon rolling down the road.

Mama smiled at Pansy and said, "Well, are you ready to help take care of a baby?"

Pansy returned her smile and said, "You mean to take care of a baby girl!"

Papa interrupted their game and said, "Whatever it is, you better get ready, 'cause the doc said it won't be long now." Pansy was filled with excitement and went back to Mama's side, patting her tummy, right where the baby was resting.

"With all the bumping down these dirt roads, it's no telling what kind of baby we'll be getting!" exclaimed Mama.

"It may be a monkey!" Pansy laughed.

The family headed from the doctor's house about a mile to a farm home on the edge of town. The doctor told them the family who lives there has rented out a room from time-to-time.

In a few minutes, they were meeting the Applebee's. They were an older couple that, despite their funny name, Papa and Mama found to be delightful and willing to share their home for a while. The family moved in and began to make ready for the baby to come into the world.

A few days passed and, one night, Pansy woke up from her sleep to hear Mama in the next room. Pansy jumped out of bed and put on her robe and slippers. When she exited her room, she saw Papa sitting in the living room chair with Mr. Applebee sitting across from him. The two men were visiting like it was the middle of the afternoon, not four o'clock in the morning.

"Hello, Pansy!" said Mr. Applebee, "This is going to be a very exciting day for the Hunt family!"

Papa smiled and put his arm around Pansy's waist.

"Mama is okay," Papa whispered in her ear. "This is just the natural part of life. It's how you came into the world ten years ago."

Pansy hadn't thought of it quite that way before. From time to time, Pansy would hear Mama in the other room, but Papa would always reassure her that the doctor and nurse are with her and everything will be okay. About ten minutes after five in the morning, it had become quiet, and Pansy had almost fallen asleep on the living room couch next to the men, when the morning silence was shattered by the loudest cry she had ever heard! It startled her from her near sleep, and then she realized the noise she was hearing was that of a new baby being born into this world.

"She's here!!!" exclaimed Pansy! After a few minutes, which to Pansy seemed like hours, the doctor poked his head out of the bedroom and motioned for George to come into the room.

Papa looked at Pansy and said, "I'll come get you in a minute." When the door opened the sound of the crying baby was tumultuous.

Pansy looked at Mr. Applebee, with a disappointed voice, and said, "It sounds like a boy to me."

Mr. Applebee laughed and replied, "You don't think baby girls can cry loudly?"

"Not that loud." Pansy answered.

The door swung open and Papa stood smiling and invited Pansy to come on in. Pansy peeked her head around the door, seeing Mama sitting up slightly in bed, holding a tiny bundle of blankets out of which was poking the tiny face of a very vocal baby.

Mama smiled at Pansy and said, "Come say hello to Bonita. Your sister has arrived."

The next few days were so filled with the excitement of the new arrival, Pansy hardly had time to think about anything else. Mama was getting stronger, and there was talk of continuing the trip home. Papa thought they could be home in less than a week from here, and Mama felt like she'd be ready for travel in two or three more weeks.

Pansy and Bonita

"Home!" Pansy thought nothing ever sounded so good.

Mrs. Applebee had been like a mother to Mama and a grandmother to Pansy. The Applebee's were some of the sweetest people Pansy had ever met. Every morning, Mrs. Applebee would have a hot breakfast ready and, all day long, she would help and worry over Mama and the baby. Pansy noticed there were no pictures around the house of children and Mrs. Applebee never spoke of her own family. Perhaps, they never had any children of their own, so this was a very special event for the old couple. Pansy thought about how sad that might be for the old couple when her family had to finally leave to continue their journey homeward.

It was at breakfast one morning that Mr. Applebee walked in from the front porch holding the newspaper in his hand.

"George!" He asked, as Papa was sipping his coffee. "Have you seen the paper today?"

Papa replied that he had not seen the paper.

"Look at this headline," said Mr. Applebee, "*Hurricane of the Century Hits Galveston Island*." More than 8,000 perish!"

Papa froze in his seat, as did Mama and Pansy. It was like a cold, dark, ominous blanket had been thrown over them. The reality of Papa's dream was sitting there in black and white on the front cover of the newspaper. A sense of panic and helplessness hit all of them.

They had to explain their reaction to Mr. and Mrs. Applebee, who were understanding, but, perhaps, a little confused by their story. For the next few days, the dark cloud of concern followed the three of them. Pansy thought of all the friends her family had made and wondered if any of them thought about Papa's urging to beware of a coming storm. She hoped they had escaped the tragic catastrophe.

When Bonita was a month old, Papa packed up the wagon again, and they headed up the mountains toward Lincoln, New Mexico, and home. The trip would only take a few days, as they rushed on toward the familiar mountains ahead.

When they finally arrived in Lincoln, they stopped to purchase supplies before they headed on the last leg of the trip over the mountain pass and back to their home. While they were in Lincoln, Papa checked the mail, which was being held for him at the post office. By now, a large stack of letters had gathered, mostly for Papa. There were a few for Mama from family, and there was one special letter for Pansy. As they pulled out of town and up the mountain pass, Papa handed the unexpected letter to Pansy. On the front, she read the name on the return address.

Annie Fox
10211 Brinkmeyer
Houston, Texas

Of course, this was her friend, Annie, from Galveston. She excitedly rushed to open the letter. Inside, she learned that Annie and her family and all of the families on N ½ Avenue got off Galveston Island before the storm hit. Annie wrote that, when they saw the storm coming, many thought of Mr. Hunt's warning, and decided to not take the chance, but left the Island. Everyone in the wagon breathed a sigh of relief and thanked the Lord that their friends were safe. Annie even mentioned that Mr. Moore was okay, although his store, like all of their houses, including the Big House, was wiped away by the storm.

After reading the letter several times, Pansy sat back in the rear of the wagon and thought about the long trip that was about to end. She felt much older than she did at the start of this trip. Pansy had learned many things about the value of family and the value of friends. She had learned the importance of keeping God close and being able to hear His voice. The most important lesson she learned on this one-year trip was that God will never leave us nor forsake us!

As they rolled out of Lincoln, along the winding trail up the mountain, the smell of the pine trees and the view of familiar mountain peaks brought back sweet memories of happy days on the ranch. Pansy climbed out of the moving wagon and walked for a while, next to Star, so she could take in the beauty of the place she called home.

As she walked along, she thought of all those people who lost their homes in Galveston. She thought of the many people she had met along the way in Texas. She was so thankful for the log cabin ranch house and the Capitan Mountains that reach out to the wide prairie below. Pansy thought how some people might think this is a pretty rustic and old-fashioned way to live. No motorcars, no Ferris wheels, no street lights, but it was the most wonderful place on earth to her. Pansy picked up a stick and began playing fetch with Star.

They climbed on over the mountain pass with Papa leading the horses, Mama sitting in the back of the wagon on pillows holding Bonita, and Pansy walking with Star at her side.

As the light was fading just beyond the mountain range to the West, they could see the familiar frame of their log cabin ranch house glowing from the redness of the setting sun. Pansy had never seen anything that looked so beautiful in her life. Even Star recognized the familiar sight, jumped out of the wagon, and ran like a bullet up the path that led to home.

Log Cabin Ranch House
Rod Hitchcock, Artist

Glossary

Alamo: The **Battle of the Alamo** (February 23 – March 6, 1836) was a pivotal event in the Texas Revolution. Following a 13-day siege, Mexican troops under President General Antonio López de Santa Anna launched an assault on the Alamo Mission near San Antonio de Béxar (modern-day San Antonio, Texas, USA). All of the Texian defenders were killed. Santa Anna's perceived cruelty during the battle inspired many Texians—both Texas settlers and adventurers from the United States—to join the Texian Army. Buoyed by a desire for revenge, the Texians defeated the Mexican Army at the Battle of San Jacinto, on April 21, 1836, ending the revolution. (Chapter 7)

Alonzo Hunt: Father of George Alonzo Hunt (Pansy's Father). Alonzo was a bit of a character. Among other things, he was known for his amazing physical shape even in his later years. He often would show off his abilities with cartwheels, flips, and hand springs. The family has photos of Alonzo doing a back flip in his 90s at a family reunion. He arrived at the reunion on a motorcycle. He was a free spirit! (Chapter 19)

American Bulldog: The American Bulldog is a breed of working dog that was developed in the United States. They are descended from working-type bulldogs found commonly on ranches and farms in the Southern and Midwestern parts of the United States. (Chapter 1)

Aunt Virginia: The character "Aunt Virginia" in this book is fictional. The stories concerning her life are actually the real history of my

Grandmother, Pansy Virginia Hunt Rule. Most of the stories in this book are true accounts of her life or that of her family. (Chapter 8)

Billy the Kid: A western outlaw who became famous in cheap kids' magazines or five-cent novels during the late nineteenth and early twentieth centuries. Billy the Kid (William Bonney McCarty, Jr.) was born 1860-62 and shot and killed July14, 1881 by lawmen after becoming involved in the Lincoln County range wars of the 1860s. My great grandfather was a neighbor to Frank Coe, Billy's employer. Great grandfather never saw this young "Kid" as a hero but as an unfortunate misfit who died a tragic early death. He was never impressed with the way writers used the "Kid's" life to make money. Later movies were made in Hollywood, but George Hunt never put any stock in the stories. He called them mostly lies. (Chapter 16)

Blockhouse: A fortified structure from which soldiers could safely protect those inside and fire upon approaching intruders. (Chapter 6)

Borrowed money from the bank: Running a successful farm requires large amounts of money (Capital) which, many times, farmers did not have. Banks would loan the farmer money to buy seed, tractors, or other machinery required to grow crops. The bank might even loan the farmer money to live on until he could sell his crop at the (Market). Once the farmer sold his crop, he could pay back the money he owed the bank and put the rest in his own savings account. In the story, many of the farmers around Aunt Virginia were selling their crops or cattle and not paying back the bank but just living off the money they owed the bank. This was cheating the bank and Virginia would not participate in that kind of activity. (Chapter 10)

Buffalo Bill's Wild West Show: William Frederick Cody was born on February 26, 1846, on a farm just outside of Le Claire, Iowa. In 1883, in the area of North Platte, Nebraska, Cody founded "Buffalo

Bill's Wild West," a circus-like attraction that toured annually. With his show, Cody traveled throughout the United States and Europe and made many contacts. In 1893, Cody changed the title to "Buffalo Bill's Wild West and Congress of Rough Riders of the World." The show began with a parade on horseback, with participants from horse-culture groups that included U.S. and other military, American Indians, and performers from all over the world in their best attire. Turks, Gauchos, Arabs, Mongols, and Georgians displayed their distinctive horses and colorful costumes. Visitors would see main events, feats of skill, staged races, and sideshows. Many historical western figures participated in the show. For example, Sitting Bull, a Hunkpapa Lakota Indian Chief, appeared with a band of twenty of his braves. The show was, more or less, the last remaining part of the Wild West. As part of the show, the cowboys, who were more like actors, would pretend to chase a bad guy who would be doing all sorts of tricks from the back of his horse, trying to get away. The good guys would rope him or pretend to shoot him. There were also clowns and other acts plus booths where you could test your own skills at shooting against that of the experts for a nickel. (Chapters 9 &19)

Capitan: The Capitan Mountains are a mountain range in Lincoln County, in south-central New Mexico in the southwestern United States. The range is about 20 miles (32 kilometers (km)) long from east to west and about 6 miles (10 km) wide. The highest peak reaches 10,201 feet. (Chapter 1)

Cholera: A disease which kills swine, such as pigs. (Chapter 20)

Circuit-riding preacher: In the early days of America, there were ministers who served several churches at one time by rotating week-to-week from one location to another. This was due to a shortage of available trained pastors. In time, there were enough ministers to supply most all of the pulpits and this practice ceased. (Chapter 4)

Cody and Hickok: William Cody and Bill Hickok served in the army along with my Great Great Grandfather Alonzo Hunt. They worked for the army as Scouts among the Indian tribes in Kansas after the Civil War. Alonzo (Pansy's Grandfather) often told a story of playing cards in Coffeyville, Kansas, with Cody and Hickok. Hickok lost a watch in the game to a fourth player and he warned him that if he saw the watch on him, he would shoot him. The next day, the man was wearing Hickok's watch in public so, true to his word, Wild Bill shot him . . . or so goes the legend. (Chapter 19)

Community campground: In my research for the book, I learned that many towns along these early American roads had campgrounds much like modern recreational vehicle parks complete with shower facilities, picnic tables, small grocery supply stores and more. Not only were such facilities convenient, they were also safer for individuals moving from city to city. (Chapter 9)

Corral of horses: Horses could be rented by the hour to enjoy riding up and down the seashore. During my research of early twentieth century Galveston, I was fortunate to meet a very clear-minded woman, one hundred years of age, who shared some beautiful memories of life in the roaring days of Galveston. One of her memories was that of "rental horses" on the beach and a large Ferris wheel, which sat on the shore across the street from the Hotel Galvez. (Chapter 12)

Crabbing: Catching crabs in the ocean. A crab is a 10-legged Crustacea, with a small abdomen that curls forward beneath the body. It has short antennas and the anterior pair of legs are modified as grasping pinchers. (Chapter 17)

Depression: The Great Depression of 1929 was a worldwide depression that lasted for 10 years. By 1933, the height of the depression, unemployment had risen from 3% to 25% of the nation's workforce. Wages for those who still had jobs fell 42%. The depression caused many farmers to lose their farms. At the same time, years of erosion and a drought created the "Dust Bowl" in the Midwest, where no crops could grow. Thousands of these farmers and other unemployed workers traveled to California to find work. Many ended up living as homeless "hobos" or in shantytowns called "Hoovervilles," named after then-President, Herbert Hoover. (Chapter 11)

Doctor: It was not unusual for doctors in those days to come to the home of a sick person. This was especially true in the rural areas where there were no or few hospitals. Even in the cities, however, it was normal for the doctor to visit the sick in their homes. (Chapter 11)

Doe with her fawn: A female deer with her young offspring. (Chapter 9)

Drought: A period of time when, for many months, little or no rainfall comes to an area of land, resulting in a lack of water, crops, hunger, and even disease. (Chapter 11)

Dusk: The state of partial darkness between day and night. (Chapter 13)

Farm: The actual location of the farm and house that burnt was near Kingsville, Missouri. The house still stands on the original foundation in that location as does the nearby church. Shortly after these events, another permanent move was made to a farm near Ottawa, Kansas. For simplicity in the book, I used Kansas as the location of the story. All the other facts are true. (Chapter 8)

Ferris wheel: A Ferris wheel is named after George Washington Gale Ferris, Jr., who designed and built the original wheel as a landmark for the 1893 World's Columbian Exposition in Chicago, Illinois. It consists of a rotating upright wheel with multiple passenger cars attached to the rim so that, as the wheel turns, the cars are kept upright, usually by gravity. (Chapter 12)

Five-cent novels: These were inexpensive fiction magazines published from 1896 through the 1950s. The typical pulp magazine was 7 inches (18 cm) wide by 10 inches (25 cm) high, 0.5 inches (1.3 cm) thick, and 128 pages long. Pulps were printed on cheap paper with ragged, untrimmed edges. (Chapter 16)

Folk hero: This is a person, who may or may not have existed, but is famous and well liked by people. Usually, it is someone who helped the common people or fought against the authorities. (Chapter 16)

Fork in the road: A place where a single road splits into two roads going different directions. (Chapter 11)

Foundation: The house still stands on the original foundation in that location as does the nearby church. (Chapter 8)

Foundered: To sink. (Chapter 13)

Frank Coe: My great grandfather was a neighbor to Frank Coe, who employed William Bonney McCarty, better known as Billy the Kid. Mr. Coe told my great grandfather stories about young William. He never saw this young man as a hero, but as an unfortunate misfit who died a tragic early death. (Chapter16)

Gauntlet: A form of physical punishment wherein a captive is to run between two rows—a gauntlet—of soldiers or Indian braves who repeatedly strike the prisoner. The word is derived from the word "challenge." (Chapter 4)

Grasshoppers: In the 1930s, there were enormous infestations of locust, which invaded the dry, waterless Midwest and Southwest parts of the United States. (Chapter 10)

Green corn: When corn first begins to develop before it is ripe, it is called green or unripe corn. Although mature ripened corn was excellent nutrition for the cattle, this green unripe corn was considered harmful even deadly to livestock. Modern testing has proven that this is probably not the case; however, the point of the story was that

Virginia was trusting God with the knowledge she had as was the banker. Harmful or not it was her faith that saw her through and her character that is seen in the story. (Chapter 10)

Home remedies: Before doctors or prescription drugs were easily available, people created home cures and home remedies. Some of these were actually very effective, but many did not cure the sickness. (Chapter 11)

Horse soldiers: Cavalry soldiers who are trained to ride and fight from horses. (Chapter 5)

Hotel Galvez: A historic hotel, which still sits on the shore of the Gulf of Mexico in Galveston, Texas. During my research of early twentieth century Galveston, I was fortunate to meet a very clear minded woman, one-hundred years of age, who shared some beautiful memories of life in the roaring days of Galveston. One of her memories was that of "rental horses" on the beach and a large Ferris wheel, which sat on the shore across the street from the Hotel Galvez. Her fondest memory was of ballroom dances in the beautiful glass, round ballroom at the Hotel Galvez, wearing lovely gowns, and walking from the ballroom across the street to ride the Ferris wheel barefoot in the sand. As she told the story, it was like being swept back to those days and reliving the joy of her youth. It was a very beautiful moment! (Chapter 12)

Hurricane Of The Century Hits Galveston Island: In 1900, the worst hurricane disaster in history struck Galveston Island. Over 8,000 people lost their lives. The disaster destroyed the powerful port empire that had existed there for nearly one hundred years. The Hunts were safely away when the storm arrived. Had they remained on the Island, they might have perished, as was the fate of so many. (Chapter 20)

". . . I will never leave you nor forsake you:" A promise of God found in Hebrews 13:5 of the English Standard Version Bible. (Chapter 4)

Iroquois: The Iroquois, also known as the Haudenosaunee or the "People of the Longhouse," are a league of several nations and tribes of indigenous people of North America. (Chapter 4)

Lean to: A roof with a single slope. (Chapter 13)

Lolotea: In English, the name Lolotea means "gift from God." The name Lolotea originated, as an American Indian name. The name Lolotea is most often used as a female name. Unfortunately, the actual name of the Indian woman who helped Pansy has been forever lost. I selected what I felt was an appropriate name for this woman who played a significant role in the preservation of our family. (Chapter 4)

Longhouse: A long, communal dwelling, especially of certain native American peoples. (Chapter 4)

Moore Brothers Feed & Supplies: According to the Galveston City archives, George A. Hunt worked for this store as a clerk for a short time during the year of 1900. The store was located at the corner of 19th and D Street in Galveston, Texas. (Chapter 12)

Motherly way: Gentlemen, in the early twentieth century, often used this term as a kind and proper way of referring to a woman who was expecting a baby. (Chapter 12)

Mr. Hunt: George Alonzo Hunt, Pansy's Father. (Chapter 1)

Mr. McCue: Mr. McCue was a friend and neighbor of George A. Hunt. In those days, when a neighbor left town on business, his friends would look after things for him until he returned. Mr. Hunt had, no doubt, done the same for Mr. McCue at other times. This same neighborly culture still exists today, but mostly in rural and small town settings. (Chapter 1)

Mush: Sometimes called **coosh** — is a thick cornmeal pudding (or porridge) usually boiled in water or milk. It is often allowed to set, or gel into a semi solid, then cut into flat squares or rectangles, and pan fried. Usage is especially common in the eastern and southeastern United States. It was often used to feed poor families because it is cheap and filling. (Chapter 17)

Overcomers: "To him that overcometh will I grant to sit with me in my throne, even as I also overcame, and am set down with my Father in his throne. Found in Revelation 3:21 King James Version Bible. (Chapter 5)

Pansy: Pansy Virginia Hunt Rule is the grandmother of this author. Most of the stories in this book are true accounts of her life or that of her family. (Chapter 1)

Round ballroom: The round ballroom was in the Hotel Galvez on Galveston Island. In my research of Galveston Island in the late 1800's, I met a lady who had just celebrated her 100th birthday. She told me her fondest memory was of dances in the beautiful glass, round ballroom, wearing lovely gowns, and walking from the ballroom across the street to ride the Ferris wheel barefoot in the sand. (Chapter 12)

Roy Bean: Better known as Judge Roy Bean. In the late 1800s, Roy Bean was appointed a Judge over the southwestern part of Texas west of the Pecos River. This was rugged, wild, and unsettled country filled with outlaws and some rough characters. When it came to rough characters, none was any rougher than the Judge. He held court in a saloon and required his jury members to buy a beer every time there was a recess in the trial. He was also known as the hanging judge because he could be merciless. He was well into his late 70s the year Pansy's family traveled through his jurisdiction. He continued to hold court until his death in 1907. (Chapter 19)

Scouts: For more than one hundred years after the birth of the United States, Indians served as an important part of the military as scouts, guides, and informants to the U.S. Army as they pushed west. Some scouts found work after they left the military by assisting wagon trains as they moved west or in the private hire of individuals such as the Nancy Ross family. (Chapter 6)

Shops and Merchants: A shop is a retail business that sells merchandise and sometimes service. The merchant is the businessperson who trades in commodities produced by others, in order to earn a profit by sales from the place of business. (Chapter 12)

Silver City: Silver City is a town in Grant County, New Mexico, in the United States. As of the 2000 census, the town population was 10,545. It is the county seat of Grant County. The city is the home of Western New Mexico University. Silver City was founded in the summer of 1870. The founding of the town occurred shortly after the discovery of silver ore deposits. The town's violent crime rate was substantial during the 1870s. Grant County Sheriff, Harvey Whitehill, was elected in 1874 and gained a sizeable reputation for his abilities at controlling trouble. In 1875,Whitehill became the first lawman to arrest Billy the Kid, known at the time as William Bonney. Whitehill arrested him twice, both times for theft in Silver City. In the early days of the twentieth century, Silver City was a center of financial commerce. George A. Hunt, Pansy's father, would travel there occasionally on business. The trip was 250 miles one way. (Chapter 1)

Smokey Bear: The living symbol of Smokey Bear was an American black bear cub who, in the spring of 1950, was caught in the Capitan Gap fire, a wildfire that burned 17,000 acres in the Lincoln National Forest, in the Capitan Mountains of New Mexico. Smokey had climbed a tree to escape the blaze, but his paws and hind legs had been burned. According to some stories, he was rescued by a game warden after the fire, but according to the New Mexico State Forestry Division, it was actually a group of soldiers from Fort Bliss, Texas, who had come to help fight the fire, that discovered the bear cub and brought him back to the camp. (Chapter 16)

The Lord's Prayer: " . . . Our Father which art in heaven, Hallowed be thy name. Thy kingdom come, Thy will be done in earth, as it is in heaven. Give us this day our daily bread. And forgive us our debts, as we forgive our debtors. And lead us not into temptation, but deliver us from evil: For thine is the kingdom, and the power, and the glory, forever. Amen. Found in Matthew 6:9-11 King James Version Bible. (Chapter 4)

The market: A regular gathering of people for the purchase and sale of food, livestock, and other goods. (Chapter 10)

Three Hebrew children: Found in Daniel, Chapter 3 King James Version Bible. (Chapter 10)

Threshing machine: The threshing machine is the forerunner of the combine, which you can see being used in fields today. The machine was used to shake and separate the kernel of wheat from the stock. The wheat kernels could then be loaded up and sold at the market. (Chapter 20)

Tide: Tides are the rise and fall of sea levels caused by the combined effects of the gravitational forces exerted by the Moon and the Sun and the rotation of the Earth. (Chapter 17)

Treaties: Agreements were made between the Indians and settlers, which allowed access to Indian land for building houses and farming. (Chapter 4)

United States became a Nation: We celebrate July 4, 1776, as the day the Declaration of Independence was signed and the United States became a Nation. In reality, it would take many months before all the States approved the Declaration and, even longer, before fighting between England and the United States ended. At that time, we began to grow and become a true country. We had fought and won our independence from England. We were now on our own and free to determine our future. It was during this time, or perhaps just prior to 1776, that the capture of Nancy Ross occurred. (Chapter 4)

Vats: Vats are large tanks or tubs used to hold liquid, such as the chocolate and caramel candy. (Chapter 12)

Venison: deer meat. (Chapter 4)

1618 West 22nd Terrace: The home where the writer grew up. My father, Homer T. Rule, never shared this story with anyone until he told me a few years before his death. They are some of the greatest, most faith-filled words I have ever heard. (Chapter 14)

2002 Avenue N ½ Street: Galveston City archives show that George A. Hunt lived at this residence for a short time during the year of 1900 just prior to the great hurricane. This is the only evidence I have for this part of the story. Grandmother never spoke of it to me. (Chapter 15)

Pansy Virginia Hunt
Family Photograph

Pansy Virginia Rule

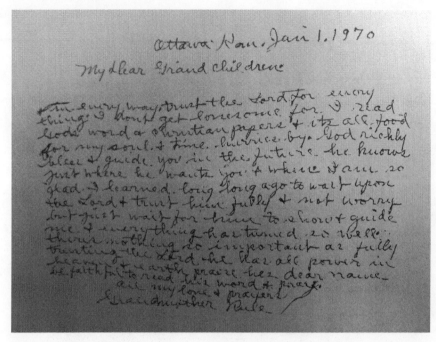

Letter from Pansy Virginia Rule, 87 years old.

My Dear Grandchildren,

In every way, trust the Lord for everything. I don't get lonesome for I read God's Word and Christian papers and it's all food for my soul, and time hurries by. God richly bless and guide you in the future. He knows just where He wants you and when. I am so glad I learned long, long ago to wait upon the Lord and trust Him fully and not worry, but just wait for Him to show and guide me, and everything has turned out so well. There's nothing as important in heaven and earth, praise His dear name, but to be faithful to read His Word and pray.

All my love and prayers

Grandmother Rule

Pansy's Husband, William Hiram Rule

Pansy and William Rule Wedding Day

Pansy's Father, George Hunt

Pansy's Mother, Elizabeth, and Sister, Bonita Hunt

Pansy's Grandfather, Alonzo Hunt

Pansy, Will, and family sitting on front porch.

1618 West 22nd Terrace, Homer's miracle house.

Letter to Elizabeth Ross Hunt
From Her Sister, Alice Darling
February 15, 1944
Concerning Great-Grandmother Nancy Ross
Captured by the Indians Late 1700's

THE LETTER

Letter to Elizabeth Ross Hunt, Pansy's mother, written by
her sister, Alice Ross Darling, dated February 15, 1944]

"Our Grandmother Nancy Ross was born in Kentucky. She was 8-years-old when stolen by Indians and was honored because the great spirit protected her when she run the gauntlet without being killed. This was our Great Granma Ross. Only I know she was 14 years old when they got her back and she married soon after. She was two days over 100 years old when she died or liked two days being that old. I don't remember which. And she has been dead 80 years. I know that much for I was 4 years old when she died. I have combed her hair and seen the scar the officer made in her head a good many times. And I have heard her tell, after she was married, the same officer, I don't know if he was a captain or a major or a corporal, but he come there one day about dinner time and he was telling Grandpa about cutting off the hand of a squaw in capturing the Indians; how he rode through the tribe cutting and slashing them with his sword. Granma said she walked up to him and with her hands, parted her hair and said, "Yes, and this is the scar you made with your sword when you cut off the Indian woman's hand." She said he jumped right up and left. She said the Indians were always good to her. That was in Virginia, I think, for they lived in Kentucky where our father was born.

Pansy (#2) at one-room schoolhouse, 1898.

Rebecca "Becky" D. Miller is a freelance artist and illustrator. Becky shares that she loves Jesus Christ, her family and creating art in that order. She has illustrated other children's books most recently Boudreaux the Bright Red Crawfish and Parker's Pickle Sandwich. Currently, Becky lives in Spring, Texas, with her husband, Matthew, and three lovely daughters Sarah, Anna, and Melody. You can view examples of her art and contact Becky through www.boosart.com.

Made in the USA
Middletown, DE
23 January 2015